The Three Investigators

"We investigate anything"

The Three Investigators

Hot Wheels

Murder to Go

||| •PARRAGON• |||

This edition published in 1995 for
Parragon Book Service Limited
Units 13–17 Avonbridge Industrial Estate
Atlantic Road
Avonmouth, Bristol BS11 9QD
by Diamond Books
77–85 Fulham Palace Road
Hammersmith, London W6 8JB

First edition published 1992 for Parragon
Book Service Limited

Printed in England

Conditions of Sale

Hot Wheels

1

Riding High

EARLY ON THE MONDAY OF SPRING BREAK IN ROCKY
Beach, California, Pete Crenshaw glared into the
engine of an old blue Corvair.

"Stupid car!" he growled to Jupiter Jones. "I've
checked everything. Why won't it start?"

Jupiter was on his way from the office of The Jones
Salvage Yard to the headquarters trailer of The Three
Investigators, the detective agency he'd founded long
ago. He stopped at Pete's auto grease pit next to the
trailer and looked eagerly at the old car.

"When you get it all fixed, you can sell it to me,"
he said.

Pete wiped a smear of grease across the giant wave
on his Surf's Up T-shirt. "Hey, this car is a collector's
item, Jupe. The Corvair was America's first successful
rear-engine car. They have whole clubs of owners. If
I get it fixed up, I can sell it for a bundle. How much
money do you have now?"

"Only five hundred bucks," Jupiter admitted. "But
I've got to have wheels! A detective has to have a car."

"Give me a break. You know I need all the money I can get to take Kelly places," Pete said. "Anyway, Bob and I have enough wheels for the team."

"It's not the same." Jupiter sighed. "I'll eat to drown my sorrows and get fat. Then you'll be sorry."

Pete grinned. "Hey, that snappy new outfit should make you feel better."

Jupiter was wearing a new loose-fitting Foreign Legion fatigue shirt and pants to hide the pounds his grapefruit and cottage cheese diet had failed to take off.

"The Foreign Legion look is the latest in college men's fashion," Jupiter retorted. "And olive green looks good with dark hair like mine."

The baggy pants and oversized shirt suited Jupiter fine. Pete and most of the other seventeen-year-olds in school still wore their old jeans and T-shirts. Kelly Madigan, Pete's cheerleader girlfriend, was always trying to get Pete to wear polo shirts and button-down oxfords like Bob Andrews, the third member of the Investigators. But that was about the only thing Kelly hadn't been able to get Pete to do.

"Look," Pete said, "after I get the Corvair running I'll find a good car for your five hundred."

"You said that weeks ago," Jupiter scoffed. "You're always busy with Kelly."

"Not true!" Pete protested. "Anyway, I noticed it was okay to take time out when she fixed you up with that date the other night."

"A waste of time. The girl wasn't my type," Jupiter complained.

"Jupe, you spent the whole night explaining the theory of relativity to her!"

Before Jupiter could protest, a loud honking outside the junkyard gates startled them. It was only ten minutes to nine. The yard wasn't open yet, but someone was very eager to come in. The honking went on in time to a rock music beat.

"I guess we can open up," Jupiter said, pressing a button on a tiny box on his belt.

The box was a remote-control gate opener that Jupiter, an electronics whiz, had built after he'd installed electronic locks on the main gate. Uncle Titus and Aunt Mathilda Jones, the owners of the yard and Jupiter's only family, each had an opener. A main control was in the office.

The gates swung open. Jupiter and Pete stared as a red Mercedes 450SL convertible whipped through and screeched to a halt in front of the office cabin. A wiry young man with dark hair vaulted over the side of the car without bothering to open the door.

He was dressed in ragged jeans, beat-up cowboy boots, a shapeless Stetson, and a faded baseball jacket. He carried a worn backpack covered with buttons and badges. He took a gift-wrapped package and a white envelope out of the backpack. With an airy wave of the wrapped package to Pete and Jupe, he sauntered whistling into the office.

Pete could hardly take his eyes off the beautiful little two-seater. "Talk about awesome, huh, Jupe?"

"A magnificent machine," Jupiter agreed, but his gaze was on the greasy bedroll that stuck up behind the seat of the elegant car. "Only I'm more interested in the driver."

"I never saw him before, Jupe. Did you?"

"No, but I can tell you he's from the East, despite the Western attire, and has just hitchhiked across the country. He has no money and no job, and he's a relative of mine!"

Pete groaned. "Okay, Sherlock, how do you figure that?"

Jupiter grinned. "First, his baseball jacket is the New York Mets, he doesn't have a suntan, and that package is from Bloomingdale's department store. All that says the East and probably New York."

"Oh, sure," Pete agreed, "that's obvious."

"His boots are run-down, those buttons and badges are from every state along Highway I-80, and the Mercedes has California plates. That tells me he came to California on I-80 without a car, and since no one in his right mind walks all the way from the East, he must have hitchhiked."

"Oh, yeah," Pete said, nodding. "That's easy to see."

Jupiter rolled his eyes and sighed. "His clothes are dirty and ragged, and they haven't been washed in weeks. He's sleeping in that bag instead of a room, and he's here at nine, when most people start work. That says he doesn't have money or a job."

Pete frowned. "What about being a relative?"

"He's brought a package and an envelope all the way from the East. What else could it be except a gift and a card, or a letter of introduction, to a relative?"

"Now *that's* pretty thin, Jupe," Pete said. "And you're crazy about the money. Anyone with that car's got to be rich, no matter what he wears or where he sleeps!"

"I don't know where he got the car," Jupiter answered, "but he's not much more than a wandering street person."

"Boy, you *are* crazy!"

They were still arguing beside the Corvair when Pete nudged Jupe. The stranger and Jupiter's Aunt Mathilda had emerged from the office cabin and were coming across the yard. The man walked with a slow, confident, easygoing amble, as if nothing were worth rushing for. Aunt Mathilda, a tall, heavyset woman, looked slightly impatient with the stranger's slow gait.

Up close, the stranger was older than he had seemed at a distance, probably in his late twenties. His easy smile was off-center, and his nose was crooked as if it had been broken more than once. His dark eyes were sharp and bright, and with his long hair and thin nose he had a hawklike look.

Beside him, Aunt Mathilda held a letter. "Jupiter," she said, her voice dubious, "Pete, this is my cousin Ty Cassey from New York."

It was Pete's turn to sigh. Jupiter was right again.

"Babylon, Long Island," Ty Cassey said breezily.

"That's an hour from the city out on the Great South Bay. My mom is Mathilda's cousin Amy. When I told her I was going out to California to see the country and get some good sun, she said I had to look up Cousin Mathilda in Rocky Beach. Even gave me a letter for her."

As he talked Ty looked around the junkyard. His eyes gleamed at the piles of salvaged building materials and household contents. Old stoves and refrigerators stood next to outdoor furniture and garden statues, brass bedsteads and empty TV consoles. There were also pinball machines, neon signs, and an old-time jukebox.

Even Uncle Titus hadn't remembered everything he had until Jupiter computerized the inventory a year ago. It had been a mammoth job, but it freed Jupiter from doing any chores around the yard he didn't want to do.

"Haven't seen Amy since I was a little girl," Aunt Mathilda said. "I knew she'd gotten married, but I didn't realize that was thirty years ago. I never knew she had any children."

"Four," Ty said. "All grown up now. The others are still in Babylon. I figured it was time to see the rest of the country." His eyes were bright as he looked at the yard full of discarded treasures. "You sure do have a lot of good stuff here." Then he became aware of the Corvair right in front of him. "Hey, where'd you get that beaut? That's a classic!"

Instantly Ty's head was inside the Corvair engine

with Pete. They jabbered, pointed, and tossed automotive talk around as if they were old friends.

Pete straightened up and ran a hand through his reddish-brown hair. "I've checked or replaced everything, but I can't get her to run at all," he complained.

Ty laughed. "And you never will, Pete. Look, you've put an alternator in the electrical system."

"Sure." Pete nodded. "You can't get electricity to run the engine or charge the battery without an alternator."

Jupiter and Aunt Mathilda looked from Ty to Pete with glazed eyes, understanding nothing.

"In this car you can't do it *with* one," Ty said. "The Corvair's an old car—it has a generator, not an alternator! Wasn't there a long, round black cylinder you replaced with the alternator?"

Pete rummaged under his workbench. "This?"

Ty took the cylinder and bent into the engine with Pete's tools. He quickly made some connections and tightenings. "Everything else looks fine," he said. "Get in and try her."

Pete climbed into the Corvair and turned the key. The car coughed once and started! It gasped and wheezed and sputtered, but it ran.

"Wow!" Pete grinned. "How do you know so much about cars?"

Ty smiled. "Been working on them all my life. That's what I figure on doing out here. I'll get a part-time job at some garage, sun and surf the rest of the time. There's more cars out here than anywhere, right? I just need a little time."

He looked at Aunt Mathilda. "I figured maybe I could stay here until I get settled. I can sleep anywhere, eat almost anything. One of those old trailers'd be fine. Anywhere I can unroll my bedroll. I don't want to be any trouble."

"No," said Aunt Mathilda. "I mean, of course you'll stay across the street in our house."

"Well, thanks a lot. That'd be fine," Ty said.

"Great!" Pete exclaimed. "You can teach me stuff. I mean, you sure know cars, Ty."

"He sure does," a voice suddenly said behind them.

They turned to see two men in suits and ties looking at Ty. They weren't smiling.

"Especially," the taller man went on, "cars that don't belong to him. That's why he's under arrest!"

2

A Real Whopper

JUPITER AND PETE DIDN'T KNOW THE TALL, SHARP-faced man who glared at Ty. But they recognized the dark-haired shorter man—Detective Roger Cole of the Rocky Beach Police.

"What's wrong, Detective Cole?" Jupiter asked.

"This is Jupe's cousin Ty Cassey," Pete explained. "He's from New York."

"Your cousin's in trouble, Jupiter," Detective Cole said. He was a small, quiet-looking man with friendly blue eyes and a reassuring smile. But he was serious now as he nodded to the cold-eyed taller man. "This is Detective Sergeant Maxim from Grand Theft /Auto, guys. He has some questions to ask."

Sergeant Maxim stared at Detective Cole, and then at Pete and Jupiter. "You know these kids, Cole?"

"Yes, Sergeant, and so does the chief."

"So who *are* they?" Maxim snapped.

"They're sort of private detectives," Cole explained. "They've helped us a lot over the last few years."

15

Jupiter handed the startled sergeant one of the new business cards he'd designed.

THE
3
INVESTIGATORS
"WE INVESTIGATE ANYTHING"
Jupiter Jones, Founder
Pete Crenshaw, Associate   Bob Andrews, Associate

"Mostly we find things for people, explain odd happenings, problems like that, Sergeant. But sometimes we've helped Chief Reynolds on cases that turned out to be more serious," Jupiter explained.

He didn't tell the sergeant that he had started The Three Investigators even before the guys were in high school. Or that the police had often been totally baffled until Jupiter, Bob, and Pete found the answers.

Sergeant Maxim stared at the card. "You mean the chief lets teenagers mess in police cases?"

"It's more like they bring us cases that we never even knew existed," Cole said.

"Well, they better stay out of *my* cases," Maxim growled. "And that starts with this one." He turned to Ty. "Read this guy his rights, Cole."

Detective Cole explained Ty's right to remain silent and to have a lawyer, and warned him that anything he said could and would be used against him in a court of law.

"Okay, you want to tell us how you happen to be driving a stolen car?" Maxim said.

Jupe quickly said, "Maybe you should wait to talk to a lawyer, Ty."

Aunt Mathilda, who had stood in stunned silence ever since the two detectives appeared, went pale. "Lawyer?" She looked at Jupe and Pete. "You don't really think . . . ?"

"I don't need a lawyer," Ty said. "It's all a mistake." He laughed. "I'll bet the guy's brother reported the heap stolen just because I was a little slow getting it to him. He probably thinks I'm joy-riding somewhere."

"Guy?" Detective Cole said.

"You want to start from the beginning, pal?" Sergeant Maxim said.

"Why not?" Ty said. "I got nothing to hide. I was hitchin' through Oxnard day before yesterday, stopped a while in a club to have a beer and hear some hot music. The place was rockin' so good I stayed around, got to talkin' to this Latino guy Tiburon—something like that, anyway. I never was too good with names. We got friendly, I told him I was on my way to Rocky Beach to meet my cousin. So around the time the joint was closing he says to me would I do him a favor and help myself too?"

Ty grinned. "Always like to help myself, so I listen. Seems he's driving his brother's Mercedes, promised to get it back next day. Says he's met this cool chick who wants to drive up to Santa Barbara, but she's got her own wheels. So he wants me to take the Mercedes back down to his brother in Rocky Beach. He'll buy the gas and pay me a hundred to do it. I mean, how can I say no, right?"

Sergeant Maxim broke in. "You're saying you never met this guy before?"

"Never been in Oxnard before," Ty said. "Never even heard of the place."

"That was two days ago," Detective Cole said. "How come you've still got the car?"

Ty grinned again. "Well, it was late that night, and yesterday was so darn nice I took some swims, looked around the canyons. I mean, what's a nice day for?"

"You just sort of drove around," Sergeant Maxim said. "Sightseeing."

"And today?" Detective Cole asked.

"Last night I slept in the car, and this morning I had to meet Cousin Mathilda," Ty explained. "I was going to return the car to Tiburon's brother next."

He smiled at them. Heavy silence descended like a tent over the salvage yard. Pete and Jupe glanced at each other. Aunt Mathilda didn't seem to want to look at anyone. Sergeant Maxim stared at Ty.

"That's a bigger whopper than they cook up at Burger King," he said finally. "If you think we believe—"

"Tell you what," Detective Cole said quickly, "why don't we all just go and talk to this brother, Sarge?"

"Okay," Maxim said grimly. "Let's go."

"If the car is stolen, Sergeant," Jupiter said, "and Ty is telling the truth, then Tiburon's brother isn't going to admit anything around the police."

"Well, we're sure not letting him go alone," Maxim said.

"You go first, Cassey," Detective Cole said. "Do exactly what you would do if you didn't know we were watching. Jupiter and Pete will go with you. Say they're friends you brought so you'd have a ride back. We'll stay out of sight and watch."

Ty nodded, then jumped back into the little 450SL convertible. Pete and Jupiter headed for the black Fiero that Pete had rebuilt almost from scratch. Pete hadn't had the time or money to fix the dents or paint it, but its engine was in top shape.

They followed Ty out of the salvage yard. The police came last in an unmarked Dodge Aries.

They drove across town to the west side, down near the harbor. The address Ty said Tiburon had given him turned out to be a bodega—a Latino grocery store—in the small Rocky Beach barrio. The barrio was an area of small, brightly painted houses and gardenlike Mexican cafés, mixed with run-down motels and seedy cantinas.

Faded black lettering on the bodega door said that José Torres was the proprietor. Ty parked the Mercedes in front of the store. Pete parked behind him. The two detectives hung back, out of sight. A small crowd had already gathered around the gleaming 450SL as Ty got out.

"I'll stay and watch the cars," Pete said.

Jupiter followed Ty into the bodega.

Inside, a few customers inspected the exotic fruits and vegetables—mangoes, papayas, frijoles, jicama, tomatillos, and rows of hanging green, red, and yellow chili peppers. The slim, dark man behind the grocery counter looked at them coldly. They were not his usual customers. Ty gave him his best smile and a friendly nod.

"Mr. Torres? We're looking for a guy named Tiburon's brother."

"So?" the man said. He was about five feet eight, scrawny looking, with a big Adam's apple like a skinny-necked rooster. His dark eyes were almost as black as his hair. He looked at Jupiter and then back at Ty.

"Tiburon paid me to drive his brother's Mercedes down from Oxnard," Ty continued. "This was the address he gave me."

Torres shrugged. He turned and yelled into a back room, "We know any guy name of Tiburon? Maybe his brother?"

Two young, tough-looking Latin men came out of the back room. They were not friendly. Only one spoke. "No one like that, Joe."

Joe Torres turned back to Ty.

"Guess not, amigos. We don't know anyone like that."

Ty wasn't smiling now. "But you've got to! Tiburon gave me this address. His brother's car is outside!"

Torres shook his head and laughed. "Man, you're a

loco Anglo. Who owns a car like that in the barrio, eh? You're crazy, amigo."

Ty suddenly lunged across the counter and grabbed Torres by the shirt. "You're lying, you hear? Tiburon told me to come here!"

"Hey!" Torres tried to push Ty away, but Ty was stronger than he looked. Torres couldn't shake loose. "Nacio! Carlos!"

Before the two younger Latinos could move, Sergeant Maxim and Detective Cole hurried into the store and pulled Ty off. Jupiter guessed they had been listening on a supersensitive sound detector like the one he'd bought for the team.

Torres jumped back and glared at Ty.

"You're really crazy, Anglo!"

"Crazy," Sergeant Maxim said, "and a thief. Put the cuffs on him, Cole. We're taking him in."

Ty stood there stunned as Cole snapped the handcuffs on his wrists. He looked at Jupiter and shook his head—saying he hadn't stolen the Mercedes—as the two detectives led him out.

They put Ty in the back of their car. With a heavy steel mesh screen between the front and rear seats, and no inside handles on the rear doors, Ty was trapped in a cage.

Sergeant Maxim drove Ty away. Cole followed in the Mercedes. On the sidewalk, Joe Torres stood behind Jupiter and yelled after the cars.

"Stupid, crazy Anglo!"

The two younger Latinos from the store, Nacio and

Carlos, stood in the doorway watching Jupiter. Pete called from the Fiero, "Let's get out of here, Jupe."

But Jupiter faced Torres.

"You know, Mr. Torres, I wonder how Ty even knew this address unless someone gave it to him."

Torres glared at him. "Get out of here, kid."

"I mean," Jupiter said, "he's new in town today from way back East."

Torres's face darkened in anger. "You got a real big mouth, you know? Hey, Nacio! Carlos! We got to teach this bigmouth kid a lesson!"

The three men advanced menacingly toward Jupiter.

3

Bob and Lisa . . . and Karen . . . and . . . !

"SMART-MOUTH KID," JOE TORRES SAID, SHOVING Jupiter backward on the sidewalk.

"I think—" Jupiter protested.

Torres shoved him again. "Don't think, kid. You gonna get in real trouble with that big mouth."

Behind the bodega owner, Nacio and Carlos grinned nastily. But as Torres extended his hand to shove once more, Jupiter suddenly went into the *migishizentai* judo move—feet a foot apart, right foot forward.

He caught Torres's shirt in his hands, pulling him off balance. He turned around and threw the bodega owner over his right side, slamming him down on the sidewalk like a sack of flour in an *o goshi* body drop.

Torres howled in pain as he hit the hard concrete. He lay on the sidewalk, stunned. Nacio and Carlos stood paralyzed.

Jupiter didn't wait for them to recover from their

shock. He raced to the Fiero. Pete had the motor running and the door open. Jupe jumped in and they roared away.

"What a great throw!" Pete said as he drove the Fiero out of the barrio.

"The *o goshi*." Jupiter laughed. "We practiced it all last week in judo class."

"Judo's good, but karate's got more power."

"When I get my weight down on the new diet, I'll learn karate too."

Pete said nothing. Jupiter's diets were a never-ending joke. One appeared, and was dropped for a new one, faster than Pete or Bob could keep track of. But Jupiter didn't appreciate cracks about his weight or his diets, so Pete and Bob usually kept their remarks to themselves.

"You think that Torres guy is lying, Jupe?" Pete said instead.

"I'm sure of it. And that means Ty is probably telling the truth. We have to get Ty out of jail to help us investigate and clear him."

"We better get Bob, too," Pete said.

When they reached the salvage yard, they hurried into their headquarters trailer to call Bob.

The old house trailer had once been buried under mounds of junk to hide it, but when Jupiter computerized the salvage yard inventory, the guys had cleared away the junk and opened it up. They'd installed an electronic lock, a burglar alarm, a countersurveillance unit against electronic bugs, two computers, and an air conditioner.

Bob's mother told them Bob was working at his job at Rock-Plus talent agency, so they called there. They got the agency's answering machine. For a few seconds all they could hear was loud rock music. Then Bob's voice, straining to be heard over the beat, told them to leave a message.

"He's probably out looking for some band's drummer," Pete said. "He says all drummers are crazy."

"We'll try again later," Jupiter said. "Right now, we'd better go and talk to Aunt Mathilda about Ty."

They headed across the yard to the office. Aunt Mathilda looked up anxiously as they entered the crowded little cabin.

"Where's Ty?" she asked.

"They took him downtown to be booked, Aunt M," Jupiter answered.

He and Pete described what had happened at the bodega—except Jupiter's judo triumph.

"Then he did steal that car!" she exclaimed angrily.

"We don't think so," Jupiter said. "We think Torres is lying. We have to get Ty out of jail so he can help us prove it. He's the only one who can identify Tiburon. Will you call your lawyer, Aunt Mathilda?"

She shook her head. "Not yet, Jupiter. I mean, what do we really know about Ty? Is he even my cousin? Before I do anything else, I'm going to call Cousin Amy in Babylon and check on his story."

"Hurry, Aunt M, or the trail could get cold," Jupiter urged. "We'll be out in my workshop."

They headed back across the yard to the workshop Jupiter had always had in a corner of the salvage yard, next to the HQ trailer. But now it was roofed over and expanded into a complete electronics shop. Jupiter had installed an extension telephone from the trailer, put a satellite dish antenna on the roof, and crammed the shop with all the detective equipment he'd built and bought.

"Let's try Bob again," he said as they got to the workshop.

"Let's not," Pete said. "Look!"

An ancient red Volkswagen bug wheeled into the yard. A pair of girl's legs stuck out the passenger window. The bug was followed by a shiny new VW Rabbit convertible with two more teenage girls in it.

One of the girls in the Rabbit was sitting on the back of the front seat, waving a beach towel. Both girls scrambled out and ran to the bug as it stopped near the workshop.

Bob Andrews stepped out of the driver's side of the bug and waved to Jupiter and Pete. Three girls in shorts and halter tops poured out of the passenger side of the ancient VW.

"We're getting up a beach party, guys," Bob said, the girls trooping behind him. "Get your jams and let's go."

"Beach party?" Jupiter stared at the five girls crowding around Bob.

"Your friend's cute, Bob," the shortest of the girls said. She moved closer to Jupiter. A bare five feet two, even with small heels on her sandals, she was slim and perky. She had short blond hair and wide blue eyes that smiled at Jupiter.

Jupiter, five feet eight and a whole three quarters of an inch tall, liked short girls most of all. But he always turned beet red when one smiled at him. "I— I—"

"I've got a karate class today, Bob," Pete said. "Anyway, you know Kelly hates big gangs at the beach."

"It's spring break, Pete. You can skip karate. We go to the same class, remember?" Bob laughed. "Come on, tell Kelly you're going to do something *you* want to do for once. When she gets there, she'll love it."

"It'll be so much fun," the short girl said, still smiling up at Jupiter. "With your friends and all."

Jupiter turned from red to white. "I . . . we . . . I mean—" He gulped hard. "I mean, Bob, we've got a new case! The police think Aunt Mathilda's cousin Ty is a car thief. They've arrested him and put him in jail. We've got to find the real thieves and get him out."

"A case?" Bob's eyes lighted up. "Car thieves?"

"Aunt Mathilda's lawyer will get Ty out of jail," Jupiter continued. "Then we'll investigate Ty's whole story."

"Story?" Bob said.

"Unless Ty turns out to be a fake, Jupe," Pete said. "I mean, maybe he's not even your cousin."

"Fake?" Bob cried. "Story? Is someone going to tell me the whole thing or what?"

"Gosh," Pete said innocently, "what about your big beach party?"

A tall redhead who'd been with Bob in the bug and stood closest to him now said, "Bob, are we going?"

"The guys have a case, Lisa," Bob said.

"Are we having a beach party or not?" another girl said.

The short girl spoke to Jupiter. "Don't you want to go to the beach with us?"

"We . . . we . . . have to help my cousin," Jupiter stammered. "Maybe later we can . . ."

"Jupiter's right, girls," Bob said. "We'll do the beach party tomorrow, okay? I've got to help out my friends right now. We're a team of investigators."

"We came in your car, Bob," Lisa complained. "How do we get back to the coffee shop?"

"Karen has room for you all," Bob said. "I'll see you all later. Okay, Lisa?"

The girls weren't happy. Bob walked them back to the Rabbit convertible and waved to them as they drove off. Four of the girls waved back. Only the tall redhead, Lisa, seemed really annoyed. Bob hurried back to Pete and Jupiter.

"Okay, let's hear it, and this better be one real

humdinger of a case," he said. "Those girls're all mad at me now, especially Lisa."

Lean and handsome in khakis and a bright yellow polo shirt, Bob had obviously come from his job at Rock-Plus, Inc.

"You're sure you don't have to get back to work?" Pete said. "On your way to the beach, I mean."

Ever since he'd quit his part-time job at the library, exchanged his glasses for contact lenses, and found the job with Saxon Sendler's talent agency, Bob had been too busy juggling work and his social life to hang around the salvage yard. That really annoyed Pete, and the two often quarreled about it. Jupiter had to be the peacemaker to keep the team working.

"Your mother told us you were at work," Jupe added quickly.

"I was," Bob replied. "But Sax had to go to L.A. for the rest of the day and didn't need me. I stopped at the coffee shop and ran into the girls. Now, come on, tell me what's going on."

Jupiter filled Bob in on what had happened, including Ty's story of how he happened to be driving the Mercedes when he had obviously hitchhiked across the country and didn't even have money for a cheap motel.

"It *is* a pretty lame story," Jupiter admitted. "But he couldn't have made up a name like Tiburon. Tiburon means 'shark' in Spanish. Now who would have a name like Tiburon?"

"Maybe the guy knew the car was stolen and disguised his real name," Pete suggested.

"Well, I don't know," Bob said. "There's a guy right here in Rocky Beach named Tiburon. El Tiburon and the Piranhas!"

4

Bob in High Gear

JUPITER AND PETE STARED AT THEIR PARTNER. "Who, or what," Jupiter demanded, "is El Tiburon and the Piranhas?"

"Not *is*," Bob said, "*are*. There're five of them. A Latino La Bamba band that plays a lot of salsa but some regular rock, too. El Tiburon is the lead guitar and singer. They've got another guitar, a bass, a drummer, and a keyboard."

"One of your boss's bands?" Pete asked.

Bob shook his head. "Jake Hatch, Sax's major competitor around town, handles them. Sax thinks they're terrible, but they get a lot of work playing small clubs and private parties. They also do relief band gigs and backups, especially in the Latino clubs."

"Are any of them older guys?" Pete asked. He described Joe Torres from the bodega.

"No, they're all pretty young. El Tiburon's probably the oldest, and he's only maybe twenty-two or -three."

"They play around Rocky Beach?" Jupiter asked.

"All up and down the coast and even in L.A.

They're about the most popular band Hatch has. Sax has all the good local bands. That makes Hatch real mad. Sax just laughs. He says he can't figure how Hatch makes a living at all with such lousy talent!"

Jupiter said, "Could they have been up in—"

Aunt Mathilda came storming out of the office and across the yard to the workshop. She was wearing a new, brightly colored silk scarf around her neck. Jupe guessed it was Ty's present from New York.

"Well! Ty is just what he says he is, but his mother is an awful person!" raged Aunt Mathilda. "It all came back to me while I was talking to her. I never did like Amy—that's why I put her out of my mind. No wonder Ty came to California!"

"What did she say, Aunt M?"

"What didn't she say! And about her own son, too. That poor boy." The angry woman shook with indignation.

"Did she say anything about any police trouble?" Jupiter pressed. "About stealing cars?"

"Amy called him a flake and said he was lazy, unreliable, and worse than that!"

Jupiter sighed. "Aunt M?"

The outraged woman continued to fume for a few moments. Then she shook her head. "Nothing about stealing cars, but she did say Ty was in trouble with the police when he was younger. Juvenile things like rowdyism and some shoplifting. He even used drugs for a while. But that was ten years ago, and he hasn't been in any trouble since. I'm sure he learned his lesson."

Jupiter nodded. "Is your cousin going to help get him out of jail?"

"Not her! She said she has no money to waste on a no-good son. As far as she's concerned, Ty's on his own. I've already called my lawyer, but he thinks he'll have trouble getting Ty released."

"Why?" Pete asked.

"Is there something we don't know?" Bob said.

Aunt Mathilda looked serious. "The police want him held without bail."

"On what grounds?" Jupiter cried.

"That he has a past criminal record and is from out of state. And even more important, he's a material witness against what they think is a gang of car thieves operating in Rocky Beach."

"When will you know if we can get him out?"

"There's a hearing later," she said. "But my lawyer wants to talk to a judge before then."

"Keep trying, okay, Aunt Mathilda?" Jupiter urged. "It's vital we get him out to help us."

The angry woman agreed, and went back to the office to call her lawyer again. In the workshop the Three Investigators looked at one another.

"Can we go ahead without him, Jupe?" Pete asked.

"We'll have to." Jupiter became thoughtful. "So the police think there's a ring of car thieves in Rocky Beach, do they? That has to mean there have been a lot of other car thefts in the area recently." He turned to Bob. "Bob, can you find out if El Tiburon and the Piranhas were playing a gig in Oxnard the night Ty says Tiburon asked him to drive the Mercedes down here?"

"Sure. I can ask Jake Hatch."

"No. I don't want anyone to know we're investigating."

Bob grinned. "I'll figure something out."

"How about right now," Jupiter said.

"Okay. Let's go."

Pete groaned. "I can't miss karate class this afternoon. It's my *kata* demonstration."

"What's so important about that?" Jupiter said.

"The *kata* are the ancient training exercises, Jupe," Bob explained. "They're the whole spirit of karate. There are about fifty of them, and you have to do a lot of exact moves in an exact amount of time. We do one a month."

"Anyway, I have to pick up Kelly at the Y after," Pete added. "She has her aerobics class at the same time."

"I guess Bob and I can handle it," Jupiter said. "Meet us back here later, okay?"

Bob grinned. "We'll tell you all about the excitement and fun we had hoodwinking Jake Hatch."

"Forget it," Pete said hotly. "I'll skip karate and pick up Kelly later. Come on, guys!"

They all laughed as Pete ran for his battered Fiero and Bob headed for his antique but shining VW. While Jupiter decided who to ride with, a sleek silver Jaguar XJ6 sedan drove into the salvage yard. A slim brunette in sky-blue exercise sweats bounced out of the Jag. She waved back to someone inside.

"Thanks bunches, Dad! Pete'll bring me home. Bye!"

The Jaguar zoomed away. Kelly Madigan ran across the salvage yard to Pete and took his arm. She barely came to his shoulder. Kelly looked up at Pete with her big green eyes and smiled into his startled face.

"Daddy couldn't drive me to aerobics, so I told him to bring me here and you would." On tiptoe she kissed Pete on the nose and grinned. "I mean, we always meet after your karate class anyway."

Pete gulped. "I'm not going to karate today, Kel. I—"

"Not going? Why not, for heaven's sake?"

"We . . . we've got a big case, Kel. Jupiter's cousin Ty is in trouble and we have to solve the case and get him out of jail."

"Case? Oh, I know that's important, but we always go to karate and aerobics on Monday. How are you going to take me home if you're on a case? And Mother expects us for dinner afterward, remember? I'm sure Jupe and Bob can do it all fine for today. Anyway, we better go or we'll be late."

She took Pete's hand, waved to Jupiter and Bob, and pulled the confused Pete to his car. With a helpless shrug to his friends, Pete got in. The Fiero drove out of the yard and turned toward the YWCA across town.

"That," Bob said, "is why I don't let any girl make me go steady, no sir! Play the field, that's the only way, right, Jupe?"

"I guess I'd like to play any way I could."

"Come on, Jupe, I bring enough girls around for you. So does Pete. Don't you like any of them?"

Jupiter sighed. "It's more they don't like me."

"A lot of girls like you, I can see that. I mean, take that little Ruthie today. She definitely liked you. All you have to do is make your move."

Jupiter flushed. "Anyway, what about finding out about El Tiburon and the Piranhas?"

"No problem. Let's go."

They got into Bob's bug and drove out of the salvage yard. Bob turned toward downtown.

"Where are we going?" Jupe asked.

"Jake Hatch's office."

"But we don't want him to know we're investigating."

Bob smiled. "Trust me."

They reached a seedy, dilapidated building on the edge of the main downtown shopping area. Bob parked in the lot at the rear.

There was no elevator in the run-down building. Only a feeble light filtered in through the dusty sky-light over the stairwell. Rows of scarred half-glass doors lined the uncarpeted hallways. On the third floor Bob opened the last door on the right. The Investigators stepped into an outer office. Beyond it was Jake Hatch's private inner office.

"Hi, Gracie," Bob said. "Is Mr. Hatch in?"

A pretty young woman with blond hair sat at the only desk in the outer office. She was typing some long list. She looked up and smiled when she saw Bob.

"You know it's his lunchtime."

Bob sat on the edge of her desk and flashed his most charming smile. "Sure, that's why I came now."

The young woman laughed and shook her head at Bob's brashness. He had to be five years younger than she was, but her eyes said she was pleased to see him.

"You're much too sure of yourself, Bob Andrews."

"Is it a crime that I like to talk to you instead of old Jake, Gracie?" Bob's smile widened. "Besides, I brought my friend Jupiter along today so he could meet you. Jupe, this is Grace Salieri, the best secretary in the business."

"Pleased to meet you, Miss Salieri," Jupiter said.

"Call me Gracie, Jupiter," Grace Salieri said. "Now cut the soft soap, okay, Bob? What are you doing here?"

"Sax has a client who wants a La Bamba band," Bob explained. "We don't have one. The guy was up in Oxnard a couple of nights ago and saw a gig he liked. He couldn't remember the name of the group. I thought it might have been El Tiburon and the Piranhas. Were they up in Oxnard two nights ago, and where are they playing the next couple of days?"

"Jake'd want the full commission on Tiburon."

"Sax doesn't care about his split on this. He just wants to please the client."

Grace got up and walked into the inner office.

"What's she doing, Bob?" Jupiter whispered.

"Checking the booking charts on Jake's wall. Sax uses the same system. It's faster than a computer—you see where all your bands are at once."

Grace Salieri came back. "Yep, Tiburon and his boys were up in Oxnard at The Deuces two nights ago. They play The Shack the next two days." She sat down behind her desk.

"Great, Gracie, thanks," Bob said. He leaned over and gave her a kiss on the cheek. "Sax'll ask if that's where the client saw the La Bamba band he liked. If it is, old Jake has a nice fat commission."

She laughed. "Get out of here, Bob Andrews."

Outside the office, Bob winked at Jupiter as they hurried back down the dusty stairs to his bug.

"Even if Gracie tells Jake, all he'll see is easy money. And now we know Tiburon *was* in Oxnard when Ty was."

"And The Shack is a pizza café that we can get into," Jupiter said. "If Ty is out of jail, maybe he can identify Tiburon. If not, we can talk to Tiburon and maybe get some answers."

"When?"

"Tonight. We'll meet at HQ," Jupiter said. "Then we'll go to The Shack and talk to El Tiburon and the Piranhas."

5

Pounding Piranhas

THE SHACK WAS A POPULAR HOLE-IN-THE-WALL PIZZA restaurant on the eastern outskirts of Rocky Beach. Jupiter and Bob arrived at eight. Pete, it turned out, had to take Kelly to a spring-break party. Jupiter only sighed.

Small and shabby, The Shack attracted students from the local high school and junior college. Most places with live music sold liquor, which meant they were off-limits to anyone under twenty-one. The law was rigorously enforced, even to making underage performers sit behind the bandstand under the watch of a club employee. But The Shack was a pizza restaurant, serving only soft drinks, and teenagers flocked to it.

On most nights they flocked. Not this night.

As Jupiter and Bob walked in they saw two high school guys playing a rickety old pinball machine in a corner. Two more ate pizza, their eyes glued to a silent TV set. Four Latino girls sat at one of the tables around the postage-stamp-size dance floor. They had to be the girlfriends of the band players because they were the only ones watching the bandstand.

The Shack was nearly empty, but the sound in the small café was deafening.

"*La . . . bamba . . . bamba . . . bamba!*"

Five Latinos sang and played a Latin rhythm on electric guitars, a bass, and a keyboard that sounded like a Mexican street band. The drummer pounded bongos and gongs and rattled gourds. The musicians were up to their ankles in cables, amplifiers, pedals, and fifty other pieces of equipment that left them almost no room to move on the tiny bandstand.

"*La . . . bam . . . ba . . . !*"

El Tiburon and the Piranhas! They pounded, gyrated, and grinned like fiends into the almost empty room. Their faces glistened with sweat. They looked eagerly at the door as Jupiter and Bob came in and took seats at a rear table.

"I hate to say this," Jupiter whispered, "but they're not very good."

"Sax says they shout instead of sing," Bob agreed. "They don't play very well either."

"I assume El Tiburon's the one in the white suit?"

"Right. The tall guy in front playing lead guitar."

Jupiter watched the tall Latino as he sang and pranced around the wire-tangled stage. Slim and handsome in an exotic white suit with skin-tight pants, a long jacket, and silk shirt open over his chest, he was all showman—a lot of style and not much talent. The four shorter Piranhas playing behind him were dressed in red and black.

"This isn't much of a Latino hangout," Bob said. "I don't know why Hatch booked them in here."

"I don't think they do either," Jupiter said.

The hardworking band switched to straight rock 'n' roll. The high school guys stopped eating and playing pinball and began to listen. More people drifted in, but it still wasn't a crowd. Suddenly Bob leaned close to Jupiter.

"There's Jake Hatch."

A short, stocky man in an expensive gray suit had come into the café. He wore a watch chain and vest over his ample belly. He had the kind of pale, heavy face that always looks like it needs a shave.

Hatch scowled at the gyrating band, and at the room that was still more than half empty.

"Will he recognize you?" Jupiter asked.

"Definitely," Bob said. "He won't know what we want with Tiburon, but Gracie'll have told him about my visit."

Hatch stood just inside the door. He looked sourly at the pounding band and watched a few more people trickle in as the set came to a crashing end. The Piranhas immediately abandoned their instruments and joined the girls at the front table. Tiburon circulated through the small crowd, talking and grinning. Jake Hatch lit a cigar. Then he saw Bob, and his heavy eyebrows went up. He came over to the table.

"So?" Hatch said as he sat down. "Sendler needs Tiburon and the Piranahs, eh? Get it straight: I don't split commissions."

"We might be interested in a La Bamba band," Bob said. "Sax sent us to look at Tiburon. He's looking in L.A."

Hatch laughed nastily. "That ain't what Gracie tells me. You got a guy that spotted Tiburon and the boys up in Oxnard a couple of nights ago. He's hot for them."

"But we don't have to find Tiburon do we?" Bob grinned. "If we do, it's a fifty-fifty split."

Hatch's face darkened with anger. "Someday I'm gonna run that Sendler out of town. Everyone knows he lies and cheats to get clients and gigs. You'll go with him, kid, if you don't wise up and get your act straight."

"Glad to see you're so interested in my career," Bob said smoothly.

"Take my advice and dump Sendler," Jake Hatch said. He puffed on his cigar. "How'd you like to make some good money right now?"

"I always like to make money." Bob smiled.

"Tell me everything Sendler does. Who his clients are, how he lines up his bands, the works."

"Gosh, that'd be spying, wouldn't it, Mr. Hatch?" Bob said in mock horror.

"Everyone spies, kid."

"Sorry, Mr. Hatch. That's not my style."

Hatch glared at him.

"Don't play so honest with me. What do you call what you're doing in here? You think I don't know Sendler sent you here to make a deal with Tiburon behind my back."

"Says who?" Bob smiled. "Sax doesn't—"

Jupiter kicked Bob under the table. They couldn't tell Jake Hatch that Saxon Sendler didn't know they were there. Hatch would realize that the whole story about someone wanting El Tiburon and the Piranhas was a hoax. The agent looked at them suspiciously. Just then El Tiburon appeared at the table.

"Hey, you're talking about El Tiburon, eh?" the tall, flashy bandleader announced. "My fans, right? You love our music. You gotta have El Tiburon and the Piranhas."

"Well—" Bob began.

"You're all great," Jupiter said hastily. "Especially you. Are you El Tiburon himself?"

"You're looking at him." The guitarist-singer drew himself up to his full height. Close up, he had a long, proud face as smooth as pale-brown glove leather. "You want a autographed picture? Jake, give these guys a pub shot."

Hatch looked dubiously at Jupiter, not sure what his connection to Bob was. The uncertainty was clear on his face. If Jupiter was a real fan, Hatch didn't want to offend him. But if Jupe was only there with Bob, Hatch wouldn't do him any favors. He played it safe by trying to pass it over and tell Tiburon about Bob at the same time.

"They're out in the car. I'll get one later." He nodded at Bob. "This guy here ain't a fan. He works—"

"Hey, I know my fans." Tiburon scowled. His teeth showed, making his sharp face look a lot like his namesake. "Go get a picture for my friend, okay?"

Both Bob and Jupiter thought Hatch would explode. But the talent agent only swallowed hard. He managed a smile, got up, and went out the front door.

"Could I get a picture for my cousin Ty too?" Jupiter asked after Hatch had gone.

"Sure, Jake'll bring a couple. Your cousin's another fan of mine?"

"Not exactly," Jupiter said. "Ty says he knows you. He wanted me to talk to you."

"He someone in another band? I know a lot of guys in bands."

"No," Jupiter said. "He's the guy who drove your brother's car to Rocky Beach for you. He tried to, anyway, but he couldn't find your brother."

El Tiburon's smile slowly faded. Then the smile came back, but it was a different smile now. The smile of a real shark.

"Yeah, I heard about this loco Anglo, steals some hot wheels and comes around with a crazy story about I asks him to drive it to my brother. Hey, even the cops don't buy a story like that." He shook his head as if sad for poor, crazy Ty. "Your cousin, hey? Too bad."

"So you don't know about the car or Ty?" Bob said.

Tiburon laughed. "Hey, man, this cousin you got should've stayed up in Oxnard. I mean, I ain't even *got* no brother!" And the tall bandleader walked off, laughing all the way to the bandstand.

Bob looked at Jupiter in dismay. "Jupe? If he doesn't have a brother, Ty has to be lying!"

Up on the bandstand the four Piranhas stared at Jupiter and Bob. Jake Hatch returned with a stack of photographs in his hand. He looked at the guys and then at El Tiburon and the Piranhas tuning up for their next set. The talent agent walked over to the band.

"Come on," Jupiter said quickly, "let's get out of here."

"Don't you want the photo?" Bob said.

"Watch me."

They pushed through more arriving people and went out into the night. As they passed the display board outside on their way to Bob's VW, Jupiter grabbed the photo of Tiburon and pulled it off.

Bob was still dejected when they got into the car. "He wouldn't lie about a brother, Jupe. It's got to be your cousin who's lying."

"Not if Tiburon was making Ty deliver a stolen car and lied about a brother *then*," Jupiter said as Bob started the car and drove off. "And," he added grimly, "someone is sure lying now."

"Who, Jupe? What lie?"

"Tiburon could only have heard Ty's story from us, the police, or Joe Torres and his friends. We didn't tell. The police wouldn't have. So Tiburon had to have been told what happened at the bodega by Torres or one of the other two. Which means one or all of them *do* know Tiburon and were lying to us and to the police!"

"You're right, Jupe!" Bob said.

"And," Jupiter added, "neither of us mentioned Oxnard to Tiburon tonight, yet he knew Ty had gotten the car in Oxnard."

"Wow! So either Torres told Tiburon about Oxnard, or Ty is telling the truth about Tiburon. Or both. What do we do?"

"What we do," Jupiter said, "is turn this car around and go back and wait for Tiburon and the Piranhas to come out of The Shack."

6

Follow That Shark!

THEY SHIVERED IN THE UNHEATED VW AND LISTENED to the loud music from The Shack. Southern California is really a desert climate, warm during the day but cold at night. In spring the cold chills to the bone. It was a long night for the Investigators.

The music, and the few customers drifting in and out of the café, went on until midnight. Then silence. The last patrons came out in twos and threes. Finally the band exploded through the double doors in a bedlam of swearing and raging and bad temper.

The surliest of all was Jake Hatch. Under the single street lamp he waved his arms at a bearded man who seemed to be the owner of The Shack. Tiburon and the Piranhas stood around them in a sullen circle. At last Hatch said something short and sharp to the band, stalked off to a silver-gray Rolls-Royce, and drove away. The Shack owner threw up his arms and went back inside. Tiburon and the Piranhas vanished around the back of the building.

"Follow them, Bob!" Jupiter said quickly.

"That's the parking lot back there, Jupe. They have to come out this way," Bob said. He nodded his head in the direction Jake Hatch had vanished in his Rolls-Royce. "That Rolls has to be secondhand, but I still can't figure how Jake can afford it on his talent business. Sax says even he couldn't."

Bob was still shaking his head over the Rolls-Royce when the first of the band's cars came out from behind the now darkened building.

"Holy cow!" Jupiter exclaimed.

It was a large sedan, what make or year neither of them could tell. It was totally covered with spray-painted graffiti from one end to the other, even on the windows!

The car was painted so thickly with messages that its original body color was invisible. It was so low to the ground that its real shape was difficult to make out.

"It's a lowrider!" Jupiter exclaimed.

The specially rebuilt car rode only six inches above the street. Its springs and shocks had been cut down, or perhaps it had been modified with a hydraulic system that lowered the whole car. If the car was hydraulic, the driver could reraise it for highway driving. The car had steel plates under the front and rear to protect the underside when it hit bumps in the road, or when going in and out of driveways.

It was followed out in a stately procession by four other lowriders. They all turned toward the barrio.

Only young Latinos drove lowriders. The cars were part of life in the barrio, a special way to be different from Anglos and dazzle the girls. Usually lowriders were beautifully kept. They were painted and re-painted, polished and shined, decorated outside and in, until they were in perfect condition for parading on Saturday night and competing in car shows.

But these lowriders were different. They were ugly, with thickly painted messages that proclaimed the name and talent of El Tiburon and the Piranhas in ten different colors.

"It's advertising," Jupiter said. "Their trademark. At least they'll be easy to follow. They have to drive slowly."

Bob gave the gaudy lowriders a block's head start before he began to follow them. He had to keep re-ducing speed to stay far enough behind the slow pro-cession. At last they reached the edge of the barrio. Bob was still hanging back when the lowriders all turned into a car wash next to a Taco Bell only two blocks from Rocky Beach High School. On a school holiday there were a lot of cars parked at the Taco Bell, even after midnight. It was a hangout Bob and Jupiter knew well.

They cruised slowly past the car wash, where Tibu-ron, the Piranhas, and their girlfriends had left their cars. Now they were lounging in the indoor waiting area, having snacks and soft drinks. Some other young Latinos had joined them.

"We'd better stake out," Jupiter said. "The Taco Bell looks like a good place."

"I'll bet it does." Bob grinned.

"And what does that mean?" Jupiter demanded.

"I never heard of a diet with fast-food tacos."

"There are diets with *everything* on them," Jupiter said loftily.

"Not tacos on a grapefruit and cottage cheese diet."

Jupiter groaned. "But I'm starving."

"Hey, I don't care if you're fat."

"I am not fat! A little . . . heavy, maybe, but—"

"Jupe, it's okay. Pete and I like you, heavy *or* skinny. Now come on, what do we do?"

"We stake out at the Taco Bell," Jupiter said stiffly. "And if we don't have a taco, we'll stand out too much."

Bob turned his head to hide his smile as he made a U-turn. He drove back down the street and into the Taco Bell parking lot. They got out and mingled with the crowd at the stand. They knew some of the kids from high school and chatted with them as they waited in line.

Bob and Jupe took their tacos to a table by the window. They had a perfect view of the car wash. The bench was gone from this table, so they sat on the table as they munched and watched.

At this late hour the car wash was closed to customers, but it seemed to open for El Tiburon and the

Piranhas. An older man stood behind the food counter, but all the car wash attendants were gone. El Tiburon was clearly in charge. He lounged in the only easy chair, with the Piranhas and their girlfriends all around him. He talked and they all listened.

Except one girl. She got up and went to buy something at the counter. El Tiburon pointed a long finger and shouted loud enough for Bob and Jupiter to hear at the Taco Bell.

"Get back here, chick! No groceries when we talk business. You got that, Owner?"

At the food counter the older man shrugged and shook his head at the girl. She whirled around and snapped out something to Tiburon. Instantly Tiburon was up and beside her. He grabbed her arm. One of the guys who wasn't a Piranha jumped up and pulled Tiburon's hand away.

Everyone froze inside the car-wash lounge.

Tiburon reached out and held the other guy's shirt. The guy knocked Tiburon's hand away. Tiburon hit him with a hard right. The girl's defender staggered but came back with a wild left of his own and then a right-hand punch. Tiburon ducked the left, blocked the right, and knocked the other guy down with a single powerful punch. This time the guy didn't try to get up.

Tiburon said something and laughed. Everyone laughed. Except the girl who had defied Tiburon. She bent down over her fallen champion. Tiburon strode back to his easy chair and started to talk again as if nothing had happened.

Jupiter and Bob watched from their table at the Taco Bell.

"He acts more like a gang leader than a bandleader," Bob said.

"Yes," Jupiter agreed. "He seems to be both. As if the band is part of a larger gang. I think—" The leader of the Investigators stopped in mid-sentence.

A car had pulled into the car wash. A man got out and motioned toward the lounge.

"It's Joe Torres!" Jupiter exclaimed.

Inside the lounge Tiburon stood up, said something to a Piranha, and hurried outside to meet Torres. They stood talking in the shadows for some time as the rest of the gang waited inside.

"Torres *was* lying!" Bob cried. "He definitely does know Tiburon. I'll bet he was the one the stolen car was really supposed to be delivered to. Tiburon just made up the story about his brother."

"Maybe and maybe not," Jupiter said. "Torres was lying about not knowing Tiburon, but that doesn't make the rest true, Bob. I mean, maybe Torres was protecting Tiburon, but doesn't know anything about the stolen cars. Or Tiburon did what Ty says up in Oxnard, but was only being used. Maybe Tiburon had no idea the car was stolen."

"So how do we find out?"

"We have to know more," Jupiter said. "We'll watch awhile longer."

"It's getting late," Bob said. "If Sax gets back from L.A. tonight, I might have to work tomorrow."

"We've got to find out if Tiburon knew the car was stolen, or if he didn't, who told him to get Ty to drive it down to Torres's bodega."

"Jupe!" Bob said suddenly.

Tiburon had gone back inside the lounge, and Joe Torres was heading straight for the Taco Bell!

"He'll recognize me!" Jupiter said, panic-stricken.

He looked for a place to hide. There was nowhere!

The Taco Bell was all but deserted now, the few remaining patrons widely scattered among the bare tables. The parking lot was well lighted and almost empty. The long counter inside the hacienda-like building had no customers.

"Quick!" Bob said. "Kneel down!"

Jupiter knelt down on the floor beside their benchless table. Bob took off his denim jacket and sat on Jupiter's back, using it like a bench! He draped his jacket over his knees as if his legs were cold. Then he leaned casually back against the table in the dim light, munching the last of his second taco.

Bob looked innocently at Torres as the scrawny Latino went by. He hoped the bodega owner wouldn't notice that there was no bench on either side of the hidden Jupiter. But Torres barely glanced at Bob as he walked past him to the counter.

Jupiter's voice was muffled. "For a skinny runt you weigh a ton. Can I get up?"

"He's still at the counter. He could look this way again any second. Better stay down."

Jupiter groaned.

Bob laughed silently. "You make a pretty good bench. Nice and soft."

"You wait!" Jupiter's muffled voice fumed. Bob gave Jupiter a gentle poke in the ribs. There was a strangled explosion as Jupiter fought to stay silent. Bob stopped teasing him as Torres got his burrito and came back past them on his way to the car wash and his car. This time the thin, dark Latino didn't even glance at Bob.

"Okay, he's gone," Bob said, standing up.

Jupiter got to his feet, holding his back and hanging on to the table until he could straighten up. He glared at Bob, and then smiled.

"That was fast thinking," he admitted. "But we'd better get out of here. Some of the others could decide to have a taco."

They hurried to Bob's red VW in the parking lot and drove to the salvage yard and Jupiter's house. The yard was locked and dark. So was the house.

"Everyone's asleep," Jupiter said. "But let's find out if Ty's here."

Inside the house they tiptoed to the downstairs den. The door was open and the room was empty. Upstairs they looked into the guest bedroom. It was empty, too. Bob was worried.

"Maybe the police have more evidence than you thought."

"Perhaps," Jupiter said. "I'll ask Aunt Mathilda in the morning. But I still think Ty is telling the truth."

"I sure hope you're right, Jupe."

"Anyway, we'll all meet at HQ after breakfast."

"Unless Kelly's got something for Pete to do."

Jupiter didn't seem to hear this last thrust at their absent friend. "You know," he said slowly, "a band that moved up and down the coast almost every night would be a perfect cover for a gang of car thieves."

7

The Orange Cadillac

EARLY THE NEXT MORNING, PETE THREW ON HIS
Bop 'Til You Drop T-shirt and drove to the salvage yard. He wanted to make amends for missing the
action the night before—and to find out what had
happened. He found the big iron gates locked, and
headed across the street to the house.

Jupiter was still at breakfast with his aunt and uncle.
He was eating grapefruit and cottage cheese. He didn't
look too happy, and it wasn't only the diet.

"We still can't get Ty out of jail!" Jupe said.

Aunt Mathilda fumed. "The judge still hasn't set
bail! My lawyer is throwing a fit, but there's almost
nothing you can do to hurry a judge. The prosecutor
is insisting that Ty is a suspect in this case. He's afraid
Ty will run away. My lawyer is almost sure we'll get a
ruling today, but he isn't at all sure it'll be in our
favor."

Uncle Titus, a short, slim man with a huge mustache, looked at his wife. "You sure this cousin is on
the level?" he asked. "That's a pretty shaky story."

"We're sure, Uncle Titus," Jupiter said. "We've uncovered enough facts already to make us almost certain his story is true."

"Now all we have to do is prove it," Pete said.

Uncle Titus frowned. "You be careful, you hear? Car thieves are nothing to fool with."

"We'll be careful, Uncle Titus." Jupiter finished his cottage cheese. "I'll go and open up the yard. We'll be over in Headquarters, then we're going out. Aunt M, if Ty gets his bail set, would you leave a message on our answering machine? We'll call in every hour or so and get our messages."

"All right, Jupiter. I'll just call the lawyer again, then be right over to open the office."

Pete and Jupiter crossed to the gates and opened the electronic lock with Jupiter's belt control. In HQ, Jupe told Pete what had happened last night. Pete laughed at the description of El Tiburon and the Piranhas in the tiny and almost empty café. He was excited when Jupiter got to the appearance of Joe Torres at the car wash.

"So Torres *did* know someone named Tiburon!"

"Clearly." Jupiter nodded. "Now all we have to do is prove it's the same Tiburon who asked Ty to drive the Mercedes down from Oxnard, and that he knew the car was stolen."

"That's all?" Pete said. "So where do we start?"

"We take what we've found, make a hypothesis, and work from there as if it were true."

"Make a what? Give it to me in English, Jupe."

"A hypothesis, an assumption, a theory, Pete. In this case we'll assume that Joe Torres *is* a member of a gang of car thieves. Then the best way to prove Tiburon's involvement is to watch Torres and see where he leads us."

"Sounds good," Pete agreed. "When do we go back to that bodega?"

"As soon as Bob gets here."

"I'll do some work on the Corvair for a while."

"Which reminds me, when do we find me a car?"

"I told you. As soon as I get the Corvair in shape. That won't be long. Anyway, now we've got to wait here for Bob, right?"

"Excuses, excuses."

"Okay, okay! We'll go now. I know a lot where people sell their own cars. We'll start there."

"We can't go yet." Jupiter sighed. "Bob should be here any moment."

Pete left HQ muttering to himself. Something about people making up their dumb minds.

Alone, Jupiter opened the bottom drawer of his desk, reached all the way into the back, and took out a candy bar. He munched it eagerly, with one eye watching the door for Bob to appear any second.

Bob did not appear.

Not that second or the next minute or the next half hour.

Jupiter went outside and looked into the workshop. No one was there. He continued on around HQ to where Pete was once again buried inside the engine of the Corvair.

"He's late," Jupiter said.

"So what else is new," Pete answered from inside the engine.

"It's that job," Jupiter decided. "He likes working for Sax too much to keep his mind on the Investigators."

"It's those girls," Pete's muffled voice corrected him. "He likes all the girls after him too much to keep his mind on anything."

"Girls can't be that important," Jupiter said.

Pete's head emerged from the engine to stare at Jupiter—just as the girl with the VW Rabbit, Karen, drove into the yard. She called out, "Is Bobby here?"

Jupiter shook his head. Pete said, "Sorry, we haven't seen him."

Karen drove out with a smile and a wave. Moments later a Honda drove in. This was the short girl who had talked to Jupiter the day before.

"Have you seen Bob this morning, Jupiter? It *is* Jupiter, right?" She smiled at him.

This time Jupiter couldn't even shake his head.

"We haven't seen him, Ruthie." Pete smiled back at the blond girl.

Ruthie looked at Jupiter once more before she drove out of the yard.

"She likes you, Jupe," Pete said. "Why don't you ask her for a date?"

Jupiter stared after the Honda. "You really think she likes me?"

"She couldn't show it more unless she asked you out herself, and most girls won't do that."

"I know," Jupiter said. "Why won't they? Then it'd be easy."

"Well, they won't. You'll have to do it."

Jupiter groaned. "Maybe later. Now, as soon as Bob—"

A third girl drove into the yard. It was the redhead, Lisa. She wasn't smiling. "Bob sent me to tell you Sax did come back and he has to work. We're going out later, so he'll be busy *all day*."

She turned the car and left without looking at the guys again. Pete shook his head as he watched Lisa leave.

"She doesn't like us, you know? Thinks Bob hangs around with us too much. She's gonna be a problem."

"Bob's the problem," Jupiter said. "We'll have to go to the bodega and watch Torres without him."

They checked with Aunt Mathilda, but she had heard nothing from her lawyer. Then they drove in Pete's Fiero to the barrio and parked around the corner from Torres's bodega.

"We stand out too much," said Jupe as they approached the grocery. "Where can we hole up?"

He didn't feel noticeable just because they were Anglo. The Rocky Beach barrio wasn't like the large barrios of Los Angeles or New York or other big cities, where everyone was Latino. Here, while there were mostly Latino people—many from families that had been here since the days when California was Spanish and Mexican—there were also many Anglos.

But Jupe and Pete were strangers in the neighborhood. Sooner or later they'd be noticed if they stood in the open.

Pete pointed. "There's a doorway that'll hide us. We can still see the bodega."

"Perfect," Jupiter agreed. "The building even looks empty."

In the shadows of the doorway they settled to watch. The morning passed. This was the hard part of detective work—the dull, slow, boring watching and waiting for something to happen. But it was a big part of being a detective.

At noon Jupiter came alert. "Pete!"

Three of the Piranhas had driven up in a lowrider, raised now for highway driving. They went into the bodega.

"They could be buying groceries," Pete said.

But when the three came out half an hour later, they carried no groceries.

"It sure looks like Torres and the Piranhas are in something together," Pete said.

"It could be just neighborhood stuff," Jupiter cautioned, but his voice was more excited now.

Another two hours passed.

Then a bright orange Cadillac appeared and parked

in front of the bodega. The driver hurried inside. Seconds later Joe Torres came out and got into the Cadillac.

"Come on!" Jupiter cried.

They ran from the doorway to Pete's Fiero and scrambled in. Pete started the motor just as the orange Caddy passed them at the corner. Pete pulled away and turned into the cross street to follow.

The orange Caddy was two blocks ahead and driving slowly. Pete hung as far back as he could. Torres had seen the Fiero yesterday, before Jupiter had thrown him.

After leaving the barrio, the Caddy turned left and entered a maze of dusty streets behind the freeway. There it drove among construction material yards, warehouses, automobile body shops, and other commercial buildings. Pete followed, hanging even farther back, now that there were few cars on the narrow streets.

Up ahead, the Caddy turned right. Pete reached the corner just in time to see the Caddy stop in front of a large three-story red-brick building down the block. It was almost under the freeway and was close to a better section of office buildings.

"We'd better park," Jupiter said, "and walk."

Pete turned the corner and slid into a parking spot. They heard the Cadillac honk. It was an odd honking: one long, two short, a long, and a short. They saw large doors swing open, and the Caddy drove into the building.

The guys approached warily. The building was the last of a row of buildings on the block. It had no windows on the ground floor, and the windows on the next two floors had been painted over. There were the large double garage doors the Caddy had driven through and a smaller regular-size door set in one of the large doors.

A large sign over the garage doors read: FREEWAY GARAGE. BODY SHOP, PAINTING, FULL SERVICE.

A smaller sign said: PARKING BY THE WEEK, MONTH, OR YEAR.

Pete and Jupe walked around the building along the side street to the next block. Another row of brick buildings stood backed up right against those on the first block. The building directly behind and touching the garage seemed to be three floors of small offices with a single main entrance. There was no other entrance to the garage building, and all the side windows were painted over too.

"Well," Pete said, "at least Torres can't see us out here."

"And we can't see him in there. We'll have to go inside."

Pete hesitated. "I don't know, Jupe. We don't know what's in there. We could walk into a mess."

"You have any better idea how to look inside?"

Pete shrugged. "No, but I don't like it."

"We'll be as careful as possible," Jupiter said as they walked back to the front of the garage. "You go in first and look around before we go any farther."

"Oh, great," Pete said.

"We can't both go through that small door at the same time," Jupiter said. "And Torres never saw you. He'd recognize me at once."

Pete groaned. "How come logic always says I go first?"

"Gee," Jupiter said innocently, "I don't know. But I'll tell you what. You go in first. I'll be right behind you. We'll look everything over before we move a foot from the door. How's that?"

"Better," Pete said. "Let's go."

He took a deep breath, pushed the small door open, jumped over the raised sill, and flattened himself against the right of the door. Jupiter came in behind him and flattened left.

In the dark there was nothing but silence.

8

Vanishing Act

SLOWLY THEIR EYES BECAME ACCUSTOMED TO THE dim light.

They were in an enormous room with thick pillars and a few feeble lights shining down from the ceiling. Rows of cars stood parked among the pillars. At the right a wide ramp led up to the second floor. Up against the rear wall was a large automobile elevator. Its shaft was enclosed on the sides by wire mesh and in front by slatted wooden gates.

There were doors at the far right side of the room, next to the ramp. At the left were half-glass doors leading to offices. There were no lights behind the office doors, and no sign of Torres or anyone else.

Nothing moved anywhere.

"You think they're all stolen?" Pete whispered as he looked at the rows of cars.

Jupiter shook his head. "This seems to be a regular parking garage. See, the pillars and wall sections are all numbered."

"So where's the parking attendant? And the service shop and body work?"

"Good question."

In the dimness, among the rows of ghostly cars, they listened. After a moment, they heard small sounds somewhere above.

"It doesn't sound like much," Pete said.

"It's an old building," Jupiter replied. "The walls and floors are thick enough to absorb sounds. Someone is definitely upstairs."

"If we're going up there," Pete said, "I sure hope that elevator and the car ramp aren't the only ways up."

"There must be stairs. Let's try that door at the foot of the ramp."

They walked over to the unmarked door and Pete pulled it open. Inside was a dusty stairway. The sounds from above were clearer in the dimly lit, echoing stairwell. But the guys couldn't hear any footsteps or voices. Cautiously they crept up the steel stairs to the second floor. Jupe opened the door on the landing and the guys peered out.

Here the cavernous space among the pillars was better lighted. The room contained cars in various stages of repair. Most of them were standing there like forgotten skeletons. Three had electronic instruments attached, to analyze cylinder compression, fuel injection, spark-plug operation, and other electrical functions. The instruments were bleeping and flashing, but no one was in sight.

"The mechanics must have gone somewhere in a hurry," Pete said. "They left those instruments still working."

"Well, they didn't go down. No one passed us as we came in."

"So where *did* they go?" Pete said. "And where's Torres and that orange Cadillac?"

"Must be on the third floor."

They continued silently up the stairs.

This time the large open area was even better lighted, with cars scattered all through the spaces between the pillars. There were more cars here than on the second floor, but still far fewer than on the first. Here the cars were having bodywork and painting done.

But no one was in sight on this floor either!

Sanders and buffers and other bodywork tools lay on the floor plugged in to electrical outlets. The painting booths were filled with cars and the air compressors were working. Exhaust blowers hummed. But no one was at work. And there was still no sign of Torres or the orange Caddy.

"Weird!" said Jupe.

"My dad always says no one works in garages except when a customer is watching," Pete said.

"Your dad may be right, but mechanics were working here very recently," Jupiter said. "They've gone, and so has Torres. We'd better try to find out where."

"You mean go out there?"

"There's no one around."

"What if they come back?"

"We have to take the risk," Jupiter insisted. "Torres and that Cadillac must be somewhere in the building."

Jupiter led the way around the large room. They stayed close to cars, using them as cover in case anyone came back suddenly. But no one did, and they were able to circle the whole room back to the stairwell. They found no doors and no other stairs. The elevator was up on this floor, but it hadn't been used while they were in the building. Neither had the ramp.

"No car came past us," Pete said. "We must have missed the orange Caddy on one of the floors."

Jupiter was doubtful. "I don't see how, but we'd better go back down and look again."

They tiptoed down the stairs to the second floor. They didn't spot the orange Cadillac anywhere, but there was a mechanic at work now!

"Where'd he come from?" Pete whispered

"I don't know," Jupiter whispered back. "But we didn't walk around this floor, remember? We'll have to look here, too."

"You mean go out there on *this* floor? There's a guy out there!"

"We've got tō be sure the Cadillac isn't here."

Jupiter and Pete slipped out of the stairwell. They walked quietly, keeping to the shadows and behind the cars. The solitary mechanic could discover them at any moment, but he was making noise that helped cover them. He also seemed intent on his work, as if trying to catch up. He never even looked up as the two Investigators slipped from car to car through the gloom.

They found no trace of the orange Cadillac.

"I guess we missed it on the first floor," Pete said when they finally made it back to the cover of the stairwell.

"Unless," Jupiter said, and stopped. His eyes were thoughtful and a little excited. "Come on, let's look at the first floor again."

In his sudden excitement Jupiter moved too fast down the steel stairs. He slipped near the bottom and slid down the last three steps with a clatter.

Both guys froze. They held their breath and listened.

One, two, three minutes passed.

Jupiter stood up carefully.

There was only silence on the ground floor—and the faint sounds from above where the mechanic worked.

"Whew," Pete said. "That could have been close!"

Jupiter nodded, a little pale. He led the way out into the dimness of the ground floor parking garage. There was still no light behind any of the half-glass doors on the far side of the echoing room.

And there was no orange Cadillac.

They searched the entire floor, walking among the rows of cars.

"Let's face it, Jupe," Pete said. "It's just not here."

"No," Jupiter said, his voice almost eager. "And I think I know—"

A sudden hissing and rattling sound seemed to fill the room. Startled, they look frantically around for the source of the sound.

Then they saw it. The car elevator was coming down on its hydraulic piston. The platform was already emerging from the second floor!

"Hey! What are you doing in here?"

A dark-haired man leaned out of a black Buick sedan on the elevator. He pointed at Jupiter, who was directly under one of the lights. Joe Torres leaned out of the passenger window.

"It's that fat kid from the bodega, Max!"

"You, kid! Stop!"

Jupiter jumped back out of the light and crouched in the shadows beside Pete. The two quickly ducked behind a station wagon. The elevator gates opened, and the Buick roared down the narrow lanes between the rows of cars to cut them off from the front door. It screeched to a stop at the exit. Torres got out, followed by the squat, muscular, bearlike driver.

"Torres was here all along!" Pete whispered.

"We'll talk about it later," Jupiter said in a low voice. "Right now we've got to get out of here."

"They don't look so tough," Pete said. "You already handled Torres with your judo. I can take that short guy with my karate."

At the door the two men stood and peered all around into the shadows.

"You can't get away, kid," the short, squat one called out.

"Watch him, Max," Torres said. "The kid's pretty good with that judo stuff."

Max pulled an ugly-looking pistol from his belt. "He ain't gonna play judo with this."

Peeking past the station wagon, the guys saw the gun appear in the stubby man's hand.

Pete gulped. "Now they look tougher."

"But they don't know you're here," Jupiter whispered. "That gives us an edge. I'll try to lead them past where you're hiding. You use your karate on the one with the gun. Then we'll both get the other one before he knows what hit him."

Jupiter stood up calmly and stepped out into the weak light.

It was a moment before they saw him. Then Torres yelled: "There he is! Hold it right there, kid, if you know what's good for you."

Jupiter walked rapidly away from the front door among the parked cars as if trying to escape toward the ramp. The two men fell into the trap.

"Cut him off, Joe," the gunman, Max, shouted.

"I'll cover this side." He headed down the aisle to Jupiter's left.

Torres, on the right, began running to get in front of Jupiter. The squat gunman moved to box Jupiter in from the other side. Jupiter quickly reversed direction toward the side offices. Torres had to circle in an arc through the cars to catch up with Jupiter, as the gunman angled toward them.

Jupiter had both men moving toward the spot where Pete crouched, ready and waiting to attack.

Jupiter zigged and zagged, drawing the two pursuers closer and closer to Pete. He acted as if he were hemmed in and trapped by the cleverness of Max and Torres.

He passed Pete. The two pursuers closed in, all their attention on the "trapped" Jupiter. Jupiter zigged one last time to draw Max the gunman to Pete first, then acted shocked to find Max almost on top of him.

"That's it, fat boy," Max said, the ugly gun pointed directly at Jupiter. "Hold it right there."

Pete leaped up, his right foot lashing out in a *yoko-geri-kekomi* thrust kick that sent the gunman's pistol flying into the dimness of the garage. He instantly smashed a backhand *shuto-uchi* against the side of Max's neck. The gunman dropped like a stone from the blow to his carotid artery.

Torres lunged around a car to attack Pete. Then he saw Jupiter coming at him and whirled to face the enemy who had thrown him earlier.

This gave Pete an opening, and he knocked Torres out cold with a massive *mawashi-geri* roundhouse kick from behind.

"Let's get out of here!" Pete cried.

The guys raced for the door.

9

Ty Untied!

MOMENTS LATER, THEY WERE IN PETE'S CAR. Jupiter looked back as Pete drove away.

Torres and the gunman stood in front of the garage, staring after the Fiero. They ran back inside.

"Your karate *sensei* won't like it," Jupiter said. "They got up too soon. They'll be after us in the Buick."

"I've barely got a black belt," Pete protested as he gunned the Fiero toward the freeway. "What was that about you having a big idea back in there?"

"It's more than an idea now," Jupiter replied. "Did you see that Torres was being driven by that guy Max?"

"Sure I did. So what?"

Pete pulled onto the freeway and they relaxed. No one could catch up with them in time to see where they exited.

"My idea was that the orange Cadillac was a stolen car!" Jupiter said. "It was delivered to Torres, who drove it to the garage. That would mean he had to have someone drive him back to the bodega. And that's just what Max was doing!"

"Then where's the Caddy now?"

"The answer is that it's still in there somewhere," Jupiter said.

"That's crazy. We saw all three floors. There weren't any big doors going out anywhere."

"Torres was in there, and we didn't see *him*."

"He can hide in an office. A Caddy can't."

"Maybe, but I'm convinced the Caddy was stolen, and that it's still in the garage somewhere. The question is where?"

Both guys thought about the vanishing Cadillac as Pete got off at the exit nearest the salvage yard.

As soon as they drove into the yard, Aunt Mathilda came out of the office.

"The judge has finally set Ty's bail. You can take me to the courthouse."

Jupiter scrambled into the small backseat of the Fiero to give Aunt Mathilda the front. Pete drove more slowly, and it was past four P.M. by the time they reached the courthouse. Inside the courthouse lobby, Aunt Mathilda introduced the guys to a tall, serious-faced man who was waiting there.

"This is my lawyer, Steve Gilbar. Jupiter's my nephew, Steve. This is his friend, Pete Crenshaw. They're trying to clear Ty."

Steve Gilbar shook hands with Jupe and Pete. "We'll need all the help we can get on this. The police are convinced Ty is part of a ring of car thieves that have been operating up and down the coast, between Santa Monica and Ventura. They've persuaded the judge to set an unusually high bail." He turned to Aunt Mathilda. "You brought the papers?"

She nodded. "What is the bail, Steve?"

"Seventy-five thousand dollars. Outrageous, I call it, but the prosecutor made a strong case for Ty's importance. They think there's a clever chop-shop ring operating, and Ty is their first arrest."

"A chop shop!" exclaimed Jupe.

"What's in heaven's name is a chop shop?" asked Aunt Mathilda.

"Instead of selling the stolen cars, the thieves take them apart and sell all the parts that aren't marked with serial numbers," explained Jupiter.

"They clean the parts up, wrap them, and put them in boxes to look like new," added Pete. "Then they sell them to dealers who operate parts stores."

"Don't the stores know they must be stolen?" Aunt Mathilda asked.

"A lot of them do," Steve Gilbar said, "but the prices are so good, they don't ask questions."

"The few parts that have serial numbers," Pete said, "like the engine blocks, the crooks ship out of the States to sell in foreign countries."

"They make more money by selling the parts than by selling whole cars," added Jupe.

Aunt Mathilda shook her head. "It sounds like a hard thing to stop. I mean, once you take a car apart, it can't be traced."

"You're right," Steve Gilbar said. "That's why the police think Ty is so important. The best way to stop the operation is to catch the thieves when they steal the cars." He looked at his watch. "It's time, Mathilda. Do you have the bankbooks and deeds?"

She nodded.

"You understand that if Ty runs away, you lose your bail money?"

"I understand, Steve."

"Then let's go. Jupiter and Pete, wait here."

Alone in the courthouse lobby, Jupiter turned to Pete. The leader of the trio beamed.

"A chop-shop ring!" he said excitedly. "Stolen cars all up and down the coast. It has to be El Tiburon and the Piranhas using the band gigs as a cover."

"We don't have any proof, Jupe," Pete said. "I mean, all we have is the name Tiburon, and Joe Torres lying and going to that garage. It's mostly guessing."

"We've also got a stolen car someone gave Ty to drive, Torres's connection to Tiburon at the car wash, and a disappearing Cadillac."

"I don't know, Jupe."

"And," Jupiter said, "now we have Ty!"

Aunt Mathilda, Steve Gilbar, and Ty were coming down the wide courthouse corridor to the lobby. Ty looked tired and pale, but he was smiling and striding along with a bounce in his western boots and ragged jeans.

"Are you okay, Ty?" Pete said.

"Glad to be untied, right, guys?" Ty replied, and laughed at his own joke. "How's the Corvair?"

"I haven't had much time to work on it."

"We've been too busy investigating the stolen-car ring," Jupiter explained.

"Ring?" Ty said. "You mean there's a gang of car thieves operating around here?"

Steve Gilbar nodded. "The police think so."

"So that's why they didn't want to set bail," Ty said. "That's big-time stuff to play with, guys. What have you found out so far?"

"You can talk about that in a minute," Gilbar said. "Now, you'll be arraigned next week, Ty. At that time you'll either be charged or the charges will be dropped. Meanwhile, don't leave the state or even the county. Understood?"

Both Ty and Aunt Mathilda nodded.

"See you in three days then."

After Gilbar had gone, the others went out to Pete's Fiero. With Aunt Mathilda in the front seat, it was a very tight fit in the back for Jupiter and Ty.

"We'd have another car," Jupiter said, "if Pete would get around to helping me look for one."

Ty smiled. "I'll help you, Jupe. Now tell me what you've dug up so far, and what we can do next to prove I'm maybe a dummy but not a crook."

Together, Jupiter and Pete told Ty everything they'd found out and guessed at. He listened carefully, but his eyes seemed to be on the rearview mirror above Pete's head.

"So we think El Tiburon and the Piranhas are using gigs to cover their car stealing," Jupiter finished. He took a glossy photograph from his pocket. "Here's a photo of Tiburon I swiped from outside The Shack. Is that the guy who gave you the Mercedes to drive down to Rocky Beach?"

Ty studied the photo. "I think so, Jupe, but I'm not sure, you know? I'd had a few beers that night. It was dark and smoky, and we were all watching the band. I didn't look at him all that close, you know? But it sure looks a lot like him."

"Wasn't he playing in the band?"

"No."

"What club were you in?" Jupiter asked.

"Something 'Blue.' Yeah. The Blue Lights!"

"Not The Deuces?" Jupiter asked.

"Tiburon'd be crazy to hire a guy where they were playing," Pete said.

"I'd know better if I could see him and hear him talk," Ty said, staring at the photo.

"That we can arrange," Jupiter said. "We'll meet at HQ tonight and talk over our plans."

Ty continued to watch the rearview mirror above Pete. "Someone's tailing us, guys. Ever since we left the courthouse. Probably the cops keeping me under surveillance, but it could be the car thieves."

Three cars were behind them. A red Nissan and a Porsche, and between them a black American sedan.

"Is it a Buick?" Jupiter asked quickly.

"Not sure," Ty said. "But it looks like a GM car of some sort."

Pete and Jupiter told him about the black Buick of Max the gunman. Ty watched the mirror.

"Could be, but it could be detectives too."

"What do we do?" Pete asked.

"We watch them," Ty said.

They reached the house and salvage yard. Ty and Aunt Mathilda went into the house. Pete and Jupe crossed to the yard. Pete stood behind the gatepost and watched the black car pass. It wasn't a Buick.

"It's an Oldsmobile," Pete said. "And it just turned at the next corner."

"Let's reconnoiter," Jupiter said.

They ran across the salvage yard and climbed onto some packing crates so they could see over the high board fence. The black car was parked practically in front of them.

As they peeked over the fence, the car moved off.

"You think they saw us?"

Jupiter nodded. "I think so."

They returned to HQ and called Ty to report.

"Okay," Ty said. "It's probably the cops. Let's wait until morning to make our next move."

Ty settled into the upstairs guest room. Pete worked on the Corvair until dark. Jupiter tinkered with some mini walkie-talkies in his workshop.

They saw the black car twice. Once driving slowly past the yard. Once hidden again behind the salvage yard fence.

10

A Plot Hatched

TY STOOD AT THE WINDOW OF HQ, AS IF HE COULD see through the yard fence to the street. It was next morning, and he was worried about the black car.

"It's out there," he said. "I can feel it."

"Who?" Pete said. "The police or the crooks?"

"It could be either," Jupiter said at his desk.

"Jupe's right," Ty agreed. "The question is, who are they tailing? You—probably means the guys you suspect. Me—probably means the police."

Jupiter nodded. "Torres and Tiburon wouldn't have known when or even if you were going to get out. And I'd think they'd want to stay far away from you in case you could recognize Tiburon."

"Let's split up and see which car they tail," Pete suggested.

Jupiter nodded. "I wanted to do some research, and someone should watch the Freeway Garage to see if Tiburon or the Piranhas show up. Bob's probably working again today. So Pete can watch the garage while Ty and I take a pickup and do my research."

"And we can buy you a car," Ty said.

Jupiter nodded eagerly. "If they follow you, Pete, don't go near the garage until you lose them."

They went to Uncle Titus for permission to use one of the salvage-yard pickups. Ty and Jupe got into the truck, and Pete got into his battered Fiero. Jupe slumped down so only Ty could be seen in the truck. Ty and Pete drove out of the salvage yard together, but turned in opposite directions. If the black car was watching, it would have to choose which one it wanted to tail.

Ty turned at the first corner. He speeded up around the next corner, made a U-turn, and drove back the same way he had come.

The black Oldsmobile was driving straight at them! It quickly parked to pretend it wasn't tailing the truck, but Ty wasn't fooled.

"So they're watching me," Ty said. "That means it's the cops. They must have been hidden near the salvage yard. Sit up, Jupe, and we'll go get you a car. Let them figure out why a car thief is buying used wheels!"

Ty drove from dealer to dealer, from owner-sales lot to owner-sales lot. He spurned every car in Jupe's price range—which wasn't very many. Then, at a small owners-lot near the harbor, Ty spotted a ten-year-old Honda Civic.

The owner of the little two-door hatchback needed money and was asking exactly five hundred dollars. He said the car had a rebuilt engine with less than twenty thousand miles on it. Ty examined the engine, took the car out for a drive with Jupiter, and pronounced that it did indeed have a new rebuilt engine and was a good buy.

Jupiter made the deal. The car would be ready to be picked up the next day after the paperwork and some small repairs Ty wanted were completed. The owner promised to replace a missing window crank and a burned-out overhead light. Jupiter was so excited he could barely talk. He touched the little blue and white car with awe.

"It's all mine. Can't I drive it off now?"

Ty laughed. "Better let the owner make those repairs. We can take the truck to your research. Where do we go, Jupe?"

Jupiter grinned. "Police headquarters."

•   •   •

Pete took back streets down to the Freeway Garage. He saw no sign of the black Oldsmobile. To be safe, he parked behind a lumberyard two blocks away. He walked to the garage and settled behind a fence surrounding the vacant lot across the street.

Hours passed with cars going in for service or to be painted or just to park. They stopped outside the garage and gave a couple of honks until the doors opened. The garage attendant on duty at the door was Max, Torres's gun-toting companion of the day before. Pete tried to decide if some of the cars were stolen. Some of the drivers who came out right away, as if they had just parked inside, didn't look much like businessmen. But Pete had no real reason to think the cars they had driven in were stolen.

Until he saw a gray BMW sedan.

The driver looked carefully up and down the street before honking: one long, two short, a long, and a short. The doors opened and he drove the BMW in.

The driver was Joe Torres.

Pete left his post and ran back to his Fiero. He drove closer to the garage and parked where he could watch the door.

Ten minutes later the black Buick appeared with two men in it. They drove past Pete without seeing him. The man in the passenger seat was Torres.

Pete pulled out and went after the Buick.

♦   ♦   ♦

Ty laughed as he parked in the lot of Rocky Beach's police headquarters. "The cops in the Olds're gonna be real confused."

"Look!" Jupiter said.

The black Oldsmobile cruised past, hesitating as if its occupants were staring in disbelief.

"What are we doing here anyway?" Ty wanted to know as they walked into police headquarters.

"If Tiburon and the Piranhas are stealing cars when they go out of town on their gigs, there should be a lot of reports of stolen cars where they play."

"That'd figure," Ty said, nodding. "How do we get the reports?"

Jupiter grinned. "Watch me."

He asked for Sergeant Cota and was directed along a busy corridor to the police computer room. A short, dark-haired officer sat at the computer console.

"Jupiter! Come on in."

Sergeant Cota and Jupiter were fellow computer buffs. Jupe often dropped in at the station to talk computers with him.

After admiring the sergeant's new laser printer, Jupe said, "This is my cousin Ty. He's out from the East helping us on a case."

Sergeant Cota looked at Ty for a moment, then smiled. "Nice to meet you. So, what can I do for you, Jupe?"

"I'm doing a car-theft report," Jupiter told him. "I need a readout on all stolen cars reported from Santa Monica up to Ventura in the last month."

"Sure, no problem."

The sergeant punched various keys on the computer to relay his commands, and after a short wait, his printer began spewing out pages. It printed for nearly three minutes!

"Is that a lot of stolen cars?" Ty asked.

Sergeant Cota nodded. "We think there's a new ring operating, but there's always a lot of car thefts. We're an automobile country." He gave Jupiter the printout.

"Thanks, Sergeant."

"No sweat, Jupiter."

Outside, they hurried to the pickup. There was no sign of the black Olds, but as they drove off it appeared far behind them.

"They don't know we spotted them," Ty said. "We'll keep it that way. Let them tail us until we have to lose them."

He headed for the salvage yard.

◆   ◆   ◆

The black Buick did not take Joe Torres back to the bodega, but to a seedy, dilapidated building on the edge of the main downtown shopping area. It left Torres in front of the building and drove on.

Pete parked on the street and followed Torres into the run-down building. There was no elevator inside. Only a feeble light filtered in through the dusty skylight over the stairwell. Torres went up to the third floor. Rows of scarred half-glass doors lined the uncarpeted hallways. Torres opened the last door on the right and went in.

The lettering on the door read: JAKE HATCH, TALENT & BOOKINGS.

Pete hurried back down the stairs to his Fiero and drove off toward the salvage yard. He watched for the black Olds but saw no sign of it.

"Jupe!" he shouted as he leaped out of the Fiero and ran to the workshop. Inside, Jupiter and Ty were studying a long computer printout. "Torres came to the garage with another car! I tailed him—"

Jupiter whirled around. "Pete! I've got a car! A real little beaut, right, Ty? It's got a new engine, and—"

"Great, Jupe, but listen—"

"—it's only a Honda Civic. I'd hoped to get a bigger car, but it gives us three cars, so—"

"Torres went to Jake Hatch's office!"

"—white with a big blue stripe, and I get it to-morrow . . ." Jupiter stopped. "What? Torres went where?"

"Jake Hatch's office!"

Ty said, "Hatch—is that the agent guy?"

The others nodded.

"Now you're making some connections," Ty said.

"So what do we do?" Pete said. "Tail Hatch?"

"Perhaps later," Jupiter said. "First we've got to check this computer printout against all the places Tiburon and the Piranhas played this month."

"How are we going to do that?" Pete asked.

"That's easy," Bob's voice said behind them.

They'd been so busy talking, they hadn't even heard Bob come into the workshop.

"Tell us how it's so easy," Pete demanded.

"We sneak into Jake Hatch's office and check his band schedule!" Bob grinned.

"If he catches us," Jupiter warned, "our chances of helping Ty are just about zero."

"I'll call Gracie and find out where he'll be tonight. He always watches his bands, just like Sax. We'll know when to show up and how much time we have. I'll take Gracie out for a pizza or something and leave the door unlocked so you and Pete don't even have to bust in."

Pete reddened. "Sorry, guys. I'm taking Kelly to a movie tonight."

"I'll go with Jupe," Ty said.

"What about the police?"

"Police?" Bob said.

Jupiter explained about the black Oldsmobile.

"We'll have to shake them," Ty said. "They'll know we're on to them. But I guess this is the time to do it."

Bob went into HQ to call Grace Salieri.

◆　　◆　　◆

Jupiter and Ty sat in the pickup across from the shabby building on the edge of downtown. Bob had made his date with Grace Salieri. Ty and Jupiter had left the black Olds looking for them in the back streets near the harbor. Jake Hatch was safely up the coast in Port Hueneme observing a punk band, and would not be back before ten P.M. Jupiter and Ty could make their move as soon as Bob emerged.

"There he is," Jupiter said.

Bob came out with Grace Salieri on his arm. She was laughing as if it were a good joke that she was going out with someone Bob's age. But she held his arm with both hands and seemed to be enjoying herself. As soon as they had disappeared toward the center of town, Ty and Jupiter crossed the street and entered the building. Most of the windows were dark, but lights were on in the stairwell and corridors.

On the third floor they found Hatch's office dark, the Yale lock open. The band charts for the month were on the wall. Jupiter called out the dates and locations of Tiburon and the Piranhas' gigs. Ty checked them against the computer printout of car thefts.

Jupiter stopped. Ty looked up. "Cars were stolen almost every place and day Tiburon and the Piranhas played the whole month. I'm convinced, Jupiter."

"But will the police be?"

Ty shook his head. "I don't think so."

"Neither do I. I think we'll have to catch them red-handed. I just want to try one more thing. I'm going to call out some random gigs of Hatch's other bands. See if cars were stolen at those times and places, too."

Jupiter called out the gigs, Ty checked, and the results were the same—cars had been stolen almost every place any of Jake Hatch's bands appeared.

"Hatch is involved. Maybe behind the whole operation," Ty said. "No doubt now."

"But we still can't prove it."

"Okay, what next?"

Jupiter looked back at the charts of the bands. "The Piranhas are playing tonight at the Lemon Tree Lounge. It's in Topanga Canyon, near Malibu. We'll go up there. Maybe we'll be able to wrap up the case tonight."

11

No Bumps in the Night

WHEN BOB RETURNED TO HQ AFTER HIS DATE WITH Gracie, Ty and Jupiter were waiting. They told him what they had found.

"The Lemon Tree? Yeah, it's a roadhouse club in the woods out in Topanga Canyon. It's pretty big for the Piranhas. We can't get in there, Jupe."

"What if you're with me?" Ty said.

"Maybe. Depends on how much they've been raided."

"We'll take a chance," Jupiter decided.

The three of them piled into the yard pickup and headed up the Coast Highway. At Topanga Canyon they turned onto a dark two-lane road into the mountains. The Lemon Tree Lounge was five or so miles from the highway. It was a rustic building standing under tall oak and eucalyptus trees, without a lemon tree in sight. Cars were parked in an open field around it, and the music already rocked out into the night.

The place was jammed. No one seemed to be

watching the door. The guys found an unobtrusive corner in the mobbed room. The customers were talking, laughing, and drinking. They weren't paying much attention to El Tiburon and the Piranhas, who were already pounding away. In front, Tiburon gyrated in his white suit, belting out the words.

"*La bamba . . . bamba . . . bamba . . . !*"

"Is that him?" Jupiter pointed at the bandstand.

Ty studied the showman.

"I still don't know for sure, guys," he admitted. "He looks awful different up there, singing and dancing around. I mean, he sort of looks like the guy I met, but I'm really not too good at remembering faces, you know?"

"Maybe if you watch him for a while," Bob suggested.

So they watched the smiling Latino do his act with the four Piranhas pounding behind him. The same four girls sat at a table by the dance floor. Couples were slamming and rocking and doing Latino steps the guys had never seen.

They weren't worried about having to order drinks and being carded by a waitress—there were no waitresses. Ty went to the long bar and got a beer and a couple of Cokes, just so no one would hassle them about not drinking at all.

The first set ended with Ty still not sure if he recognized Tiburon. After the second set, they followed Tiburon and the Piranhas out into the parking area, where the band took their break.

"I'm pretty sure, but I'm just never going to be dead sure," Ty said finally.

Through the third set the mob gave no sign of thinning, not even after Tiburon finished the last song with an extra flourish. He ended up in a complete split out on the dance floor, the sweat glistening on his flushed face. The Investigators had seen nothing that connected to stolen cars.

"They sure don't act like car thieves," Ty said.

"You can't swipe cars from a bandstand," Bob added, discouraged.

"We'll follow them," Jupiter said. "Maybe they steal the cars after their gigs."

Outside, the moon had risen. The two Investigators and Ty waited under the tall trees and listened to the whisper of the wind. Almost no one left the club, even though the music had ended. Music wasn't the main attraction at the Lemon Tree, which probably explained why Tiburon and the Piranhas had gotten the gig.

The moonlight cast long shadows on the mountains all around. A few cars passed on the road through the twisting canyon. They heard a dog bark in the distance. But mostly the only sound was the steady rumble of voices from the open tavern doors.

Tiburon and the Piranhas finally came out with their equipment and instruments. Their graffitied lowriders and an instrument van were parked in a far corner of the field. The band loaded the van and got into their cars. There were more than five cars this time. The girls who always came with them were obviously driving their own.

"It sure doesn't look like they're going off to steal anything," Bob whispered.

Jupiter stared at the colorful cars. They stood like painted ghosts in the moonlight of the mountain canyon.

"Guys! Come on. We have to get closer."

"You don't want them to spot us," warned Ty.

Jupiter kept on moving among the parked cars. The guys stayed in the shadows as they crept closer to the exit lane. Tiburon, the Piranhas, and their girlfriends were starting their motors to roll slowly out of the parking field.

"They're not in lowrider position," Bob said.

"They wouldn't be, Bob," Ty said. "They have to drive this mountain road and then the highway to get back to Rocky Beach."

The shoelace on Jupiter's sneaker had come untied. He crouched down to retie it, keeping one eye on the approaching lowriders. Suddenly he fell to the ground.

"Jupe?" Bob was alarmed.

"Jupiter!" Ty exclaimed.

"I spotted something," Jupiter whispered. "Get down and look under those cars."

The three guys lay on the ground as the lowriders passed. In the high position, with their hydraulics pumped up, they rode like normal cars.

"They look like any other cars now," Bob said. "Except for all those painted messages on them."

"Yes," Jupiter said, barely able to contain his excitement. "Too much like any other cars! Guys, look underneath. Look at what's missing!"

Ty and Bob stared under the cars as they rolled out of the lot. The cars rode slowly over the bumps and ruts of the dirt field.

"They look pretty ordinary to me," Bob said.

"Yeah," Ty said, and then he became excited. "No! They don't have any bump plates underneath, front or rear! They're not lowriders in the up position. They're just ordinary cars!"

"Ordinary cars all graffitied to look exactly like the lowriders the band does drive," Jupiter said. "And what kind of cars? Look really close."

Bob stared. "That's a Mercedes! And two Volvos!"

"There's a BMW and another Mercedes!" Ty said.

"That's what I spotted in the dark, guys—the shapes of Mercedes and Volvos!" Jupiter said. "The cars we saw at The Shack were completely different makes. I'll bet the band doesn't steal these cars. They just drive them to Rocky Beach. No one looks closely at them under that graffitti. It's just a rock band with their painted cars returning from a gig."

He jumped up as the last car turned out of the field toward the ocean. "Hurry, guys, we've got to see where they take the cars!"

They ran back to the pickup and bumped and swayed across the dirt out onto the road. Since Tiburon and the band weren't in their lowriders, they could drive a lot faster. But Ty gunned along the narrow, twisting road while Bob and Jupe hung on. Soon, they caught up with the rear car in the procession of phony lowriders.

"If those are stolen cars," Bob said, "how did they get into the parking lot. And where are the real cars the band drives?"

"My guess is that the cars were stolen earlier, graffitied, and parked by other members of the ring," Jupiter said.

"Yeah, stealing cars right takes experience," Ty said. "Lots of cars are swiped by joy-riding kids, and they get caught fast if they don't dump the car after a quick spin. But pros spot the car they want and pick the safest time to grab it and get off the road pronto. I'd say Jupe's right—the real thieves grab them, paint them, and park them. Then the band drives them home."

"But how does the band get here?" asked Bob.

Ty shrugged. "Somebody drives them. Maybe in the van. Or maybe the band picks up the stolen cars someplace nearby and shows up at the gig in them."

"Okay, if pros steal the cars," said Bob, "why do they need Tiburon and the Piranhas? Why don't the pros drive them to the chop shop themselves?"

"Because the big risk in any caper like this is the cops're sure to know the pros," Ty said. "They're the first guys to be picked up. If a car gets reported stolen, every cop in the area looks for known thieves. And stool pigeons are always ready to talk."

"Most arrests are made on tips against known crooks," Jupiter pointed out.

"It's a smart gimmick to have pros steal them, and get someone the cops don't suspect to drive them to the shop," Ty said.

"Whatever the reason," Jupiter said, "it looks like Tiburon's job isn't to steal the cars but to deliver them. So if we follow him, we should find the gang's headquarters."

"What about the car Tiburon got Ty to drive down to Rocky Beach?" Bob asked. "How does that fit in? It wasn't even graffitied."

"No." Jupiter thought. "My guess is that it was an extra car Tiburon stole for himself, maybe after his gig that night."

Ty said, "He sure took a gamble by getting some guy like me to ferry it down. I'll bet the bossman was hopping mad."

"Since the band wasn't going to drive it," Jupiter added, "he wouldn't graffiti it."

"Jupe!" Bob stared ahead.

A large trailer truck pulled out of a side road and made a wide turn onto the canyon road. It blocked both lanes. Ty had to stop until the big eighteen-wheeler straightened out and moved ahead. Drivers from the other direction now passed in a stream, but Ty was stuck behind the big, slow-moving rig.

Finally they reached a straight stretch of road long enough for Ty to pull around the truck. He raced ahead in pursuit of the fake lowriders. But there was no sign of them. On the Coast Highway, Ty opened up to full speed. He drove fast in the light traffic of the late hour, but they reached Rocky Beach without finding a trace of Tiburon and the Piranhas.

"Swing by that car wash, and the garage," said Jupe. Ty did. But the lowriders had disappeared.

"What do we do now?" Ty asked.

"Nothing," Jupiter replied. "Not tonight. But tomorrow we figure out how to catch the thieves red-handed with the stolen cars."

12

Inside Jobs

PETE, IN A RAGGED BLOOM COUNTY T-SHIRT, AND Bob, in a striped rugby shirt, were outside the gates when Jupiter and Ty arrived at the yard the next morning. Inside HQ they sat around to talk.

Jupiter was at the desk. "I'm sure now that Jake Hatch is boss of the stolen car ring. Proving it is going to be something else."

They were silent as they thought about how to stop the gang of car thieves.

"I appreciate what you're trying to do for me, guys," Ty said slowly, "but this is an organized gang. They can be real dangerous. Maybe we better take what we have to the police. There's a lot of money in this, and money means violence."

"You think we have enough for the police to act on?" Jupiter said.

"Or even believe us?" Pete added.

Ty shook his head. "No, I don't think we do."

"Then we go on until we have it," Jupiter said. "Am I right, guys?"

"Right," Bob said.

"We go on," Pete said.

"So," Jupiter said, "we're sure Tiburon and the Piranhas are transporting the stolen cars in the disguise of lowriders. And we're pretty sure the Freeway Garage is where they take them. But we can't jump Tiburon and his gang on the road, and we've already been to the garage and found nothing."

Ty said, "If there's a chop shop hidden in that garage, they're sure to have it set up so they can escape if the police break in."

"Which means we can't do much from outside," Bob said.

"So we'll have to get inside," Pete said.

"That's what I was thinking all night," Jupiter said, nodding. "One of us must get inside the gang."

There was another silence in the trailer. Bob frowned and looked worried.

"I don't know, Jupe," he said. "They've seen us a lot by now."

Ty said, "They don't know me that well. I can grow a mustache, use some disguise, and—"

"Both Torres and Tiburon got a good look at you, Ty," Jupiter broke in. "No, I think I'm the one."

"Come on, Jupe." Pete snorted. "You flattened Torres, and gave Tiburon a hard time at The Shack. They'll remember you. No, the only one they haven't gotten close to is me. It's my job to get inside."

The other three looked at one another.

"He's right, Jupe," Bob said.

Ty nodded.

"All right," Jupiter agreed. "How do we go about getting you infiltrated?"

"Infiltrated?" Bob laughed. "Is that a word, Jupe?"

"It is now." Jupiter grinned. Then he became serious again. "How *do* we get Pete into the gang?"

"I could apply for a mechanic's job at that garage," Pete suggested.

"Too risky and wouldn't work," Ty said. "If they are a chop shop, they'll only take on someone sent by someone they know."

"A parking attendant's job?" Jupiter suggested.

"Sounds like they only use that gunman," Ty said, "and he'd probably get suspicious too."

"What about the car wash?" said Bob. "That's where Tiburon and his gang hang out. And car washes always need people to do the hand finishing with the rags. Pete could get close to Tiburon there and maybe work his way into the garage."

"Yeah," Ty agreed. "He could talk a lot about wanting to be a mechanic and needing big money. Then maybe show Tiburon how good he is with cars."

"It could take forever," Jupiter objected. "Unless . . . what if we sabotage Tiburon's car in such a way that it's really easy to fix but hard to see what's wrong unless you know? Then Pete could fix it like magic and impress Tiburon."

"I can pull a couple of wires underneath they'd never spot," Ty said. "It might work."

"I think it's our best chance," Bob agreed.

"We'd have to be sure Tiburon brought his car to the car wash," Pete said.

"That won't be a problem if it's their steady hangout," Jupiter said. "But infiltration could still take too long. We need a backup plan."

"Like what, Jupe?" Bob asked.

"One of us rents a parking space in the garage for a week and hides in the car to watch what's going on. It's not as good as infiltrating, but we might spot enough to tell us where the chop shop is."

Ty said. "Who parks?"

"I'm busy all day with Sax," Bob said, "and maybe with that beach party with the girls. I kind of promised them, and I've busted the promise twice already. Hey, Jupe, Ruthie really wants you to come."

"Ty might lead the police to the garage and scare off the crooks," Jupiter said hastily. "That leaves me, so I can't go to a beach party. I'll go and pick up my new car right now."

"Wait a minute," Pete said. "What if Torres and that guy with the gun are at the garage? They know you, Jupe."

"If Torres is there I'll have to get away fast," Jupiter admitted. "I don't think that Max guy really saw me. Anyway, there's no one else. You'll be taking a risk at the car wash, Pete."

Pete gulped. "I guess we're all taking some risk. Okay, I'll head for the car wash and sign up to polish cars."

"I'll borrow a pickup and drive Jupe to his car," Ty

said. "And then I'll watch Pete at the car wash from that Taco Bell you told me about. If the cops tail me, they won't see me do anything except eat a couple of tacos."

Jupiter reached into a desk drawer and took out money to pay for the parking. Then he stepped out to his workshop. He returned a moment later with mini walkie-talkies for the three of them.

"Pete had better put on a work shirt for the job and wear a bolo tie with the walkie-talkie in the slide. The range isn't far, but Pete can talk to Ty. And I can report to anyone right outside the garage."

They drove out of the salvage yard at the same time. Bob to Sax Sendler's office. Pete to get a shirt and his bolo tie and go to the car wash. Ty and Jupiter to pick up Jupe's new Honda.

"Meet you later at HQ," Jupe told Ty after claiming his car.

Ty smiled. "Drive carefully now."

Jupiter grinned like a kid with a new toy as he drove off on his first mission on the new wheels. The little car handled beautifully, cornering and holding the road and slipping in and out of small spaces like a snake. He drove the long way to the Freeway Garage just to enjoy his new car.

When he got to the garage, he honked in front of the doors.

Nothing happened.

After a few minutes he honked again.

A man stepped out through the small door inside the larger doors. It was the burly gunman, Max!

"Yeah?"

Jupiter swallowed hard to hide his panic, but the gunman showed no hint of recognition. Max really *hadn't* seen him clearly the day before yesterday in the gloom of the garage parking floor. Jupe breathed deeply and smiled his best arrogant smile.

"I need parking for a week," he announced.

Max turned away. "Got no openings."

"Mostly I'll be leaving the car here," Jupiter went on as if he hadn't heard. "But I will have to go in and out sometimes. Can that be accommodated?"

The man turned and looked back at him.

"Get lost, jerk."

The gunman went back inside. Jupiter sat in his new Honda and tried to think what to do. He had to admit finally he was stumped. If they wouldn't rent him a space, there was nothing he could do about it. Glumly he drove back to the salvage yard. He hoped that Pete had done better.

No one was in the workshop or trailer. Jupiter munched guiltily on a chocolate bar from his secret stash as he waited. Then he decided that the grapefruit and cottage cheese diet just wasn't right for him. He'd find a new diet. That made him feel a lot better. He went out to admire his car again.

The telephone rang in the trailer.

"Jupe!" It was Ty. "Two guys just quit the car wash.

They shoved rags in Pete's hand, told him to start drying and shining!"

"What about Tiburon and the Piranhas?"

"Not here yet. I'll stay and watch for them. How'd you do?"

"I didn't," Jupiter said gloomily. He told Ty about Max the gunman.

Ty snorted at the other end. "I don't believe him. That guy just wants some money in his hand. Pick me up, we'll both go back."

"You mean he wants a bribe?"

"Sure, guys like that always expect a little 'tip' to give you a space. The guy who greases their palm the most gets the best spot."

"I'll be right there."

Jupe jumped back into his new Honda and drove quickly to the Taco Bell next to the car wash. Ty came out.

"Shouldn't you stay and watch?" Jupe asked.

"Nothing's happening, and this won't take long."

"All right, but you drive," Jupiter said. "I'll hide in back. When you leave, I'll stay behind."

"Let's go."

Ty drove off with Jupiter on the floor in back and Jupe's money in his pocket. He'd gone five blocks when he swore.

"It's the cops again. A blue Aries this time, but I can spot them anywhere." Jupiter heard him laugh. Then he began to talk to the police car. "Okay, boys, if that's the way you want it. Hang on, Jupe."

The car seemed to shoot off like a rocket. Jupiter clung to the bottom of the backseat. Ty drove like a cannonball. The car made screeching turns that flung Jupiter like a sack around on the floor of the hatchback. But he wasn't worried about himself.

"My car!" Jupiter wailed. "You'll wreck it!"

Ty laughed. "Nah. It's a tough little baby!"

Bruised and battered, Jupe listened to the little car creak and groan in violent turns and wild speed-ups. It bounced and rattled over bone-jarring bumps and ruts as if Ty were driving over plowed fields and railroad ties.

Then it slowed down and stopped bouncing. Ty laughed again. "Lost 'em. You okay?"

"I think so." Jupiter groaned. "Is the car okay?"

"Perfect." Ty chuckled. "We're almost at the garage. Stay way down."

Jupiter lay rigid as the car came to a stop. Ty honked.

Max the gunman came out again. "Yeah?"

"Need parking for a week," Ty said.

"No openings."

"You look like a guy knows how to be treated right. What's the week in advance?"

There was a silence. Then, "Fifty bucks."

"Hey, that's only half what I figured. Let's say a hundred. Got it right here. Cash."

There was a silence, then Max spoke.

"I guess we can squeeze you in."

The doors opened, and the Honda drove into the dim garage. It parked in a row toward the back.

"Okay, you're in," Ty said.

Jupiter groaned. "That hundred was all we had in the treasury."

"It was the only way, Jupe. I'll hitch back to the car wash and see what I can do to help Pete. Be back for you around five."

Then Jupiter was alone in the gloom of the silent garage.

13

The Big Payoff!

A T THE CAR WASH, PETE DRIED AND POLISHED EACH car as it emerged from the automatic wash. He and the other hand finishers carried rags and bottles of window cleaner. They worked in teams.

As Pete worked, his eyes were constantly alert for any signs of Joe Torres or Tiburon and the Piranhas. The afternoon passed. He saw nothing but dripping cars rolling out of the automatic wash line—and Ty sipping Cokes and eating burritos at the Taco Bell next door.

Pete went on working.

Ty went on waiting.

◆　　◆　　◆

In the gloom of the parking garage, Jupiter raised himself up to look out the window. The parked cars stood silently under the dim lights.

He became aware of the sounds of mechanics working on the second floor. He could even hear faint sounds coming from the third floor—air compressors humming and hammering to supply the power to paint the cars.

He strained to listen for other sounds. The orange Cadillac had vanished somewhere inside this building. And Joe Torres and the gunman had come from somewhere in the black Buick.

But where?

◆   ◆   ◆

At four o'clock, Ty looked at his watch. Nothing had happened at the car wash. All he'd seen was a steady stream of cars that Pete and his fellow hand finishers swarmed over like ants on a log full of honey.

There had been no sign of Tiburon and the Piranhas or their girlfriends. Joe Torres had not appeared. It was almost time to go and pick up the Honda and Jupiter.

Soon they would all have to quit for the day.

◆   ◆   ◆

Twice Jupiter had to duck down as Max the gunman passed on his patrol of the floor. Jupe's watch read four thirty when he slipped out of the little Honda. He crept through the dimness of the garage interior toward the automobile elevator.

He listened intently as he moved, in case Max returned. He had seen no one else. No cars had driven in, stolen or otherwise.

Now he circled the entire floor to see if there was anything he and Pete had somehow overlooked the first time. He even opened the half-glass doors of the offices. All were being used as storerooms, or were unfurnished and abandoned.

He ended his search at the car elevator with its

slatted wooden gates. The platform was down on the ground floor. The wide shaft above was as dimly lit as the floor itself. Two rectangles of light showed where it opened onto each upper floor.

The footsteps caught him by surprise!

Max the gunman was walking down the ramp.

◆ ◆ ◆

Tiburon and the Piranhas arrived at the car wash in their lowriders. They looked like a western outlaw gang riding into their hideout after a raid. It was five o'clock, closing time at the car wash. Pete was being paid as Tiburon strode into the owner's office.

"Thanks, sir," Pete said loud enough for anyone to hear. "I sure need the money. My dad's out of work, so if you hear of anyone who needs a good mechanic, I'd appreciate knowing about it."

"Sure, Crenshaw," the owner said. "You do a good job. I'll keep my ears open for you."

"I'm a really good mechanic," Pete emphasized. "I'll do anything to make some money."

When he saw that Tiburon was looking at him, Pete left. He didn't want to lay it on too thick and make the bandleader suspicious. Outside, he walked two blocks to his Fiero.

As he passed the Taco Bell he saw that Ty had gone.

◆ ◆ ◆

Jupiter held his breath as the footsteps of Max the gunman came steadily closer. There had been no time to get back to his Honda, and barely enough time to dive beside the first car facing the elevator.

Now Max walked along the clear lane between the elevator and the first row of cars. All he had to do was glance left and down and he couldn't miss Jupiter. In a matter of seconds he would look straight down the aisle where Jupiter crouched.

The leader of the Investigators lay flat on the dirty, greasy, oil-splattered concrete floor and rolled under the car. He watched Max's legs walk past only a few feet from his head. The gunman paused, as if he were looking along the now empty aisle.

Jupiter breathed slowly and wiped the sweat and oil off his brow. It seemed like Max would never move on. His legs were so close that Jupiter could have touched them.

Then the small outside door opened, letting in a long shaft of late-afternoon sunlight.

"Yeah?" Max challenged instantly.

Ty's voice loudly answered, "Hi. Just came to get my car."

"Let's see your ticket."

"Right here," Ty called out.

The legs disappeared. Jupiter waited a long minute, then rolled out on the other side of the car and peered over it. The gunman walked toward the front door, where Ty stood in the shaft of sunlight.

Jupiter stood and waved, then dropped low again to work his way through the silent rows to his car. He hoped Ty had seen him and would hold the gunman long enough for Jupe to reach the Honda.

"We close at six o'clock," Jupiter heard Max say.

"You don't get back, you don't park till tomorrow."

"I won't need to park until tomorrow," Ty's voice said. "You have a phone I can use?"

"Over there on the wall."

"You want to show me?"

"You want a lot for a lousy hundred bucks."

The distraction gave Jupiter time to reach the Honda and crawl in. Moments later Ty got behind the wheel. When Ty slowed the car at the front door, Max the gunman leaned in.

"Six o'clock, or wait until tomorrow."

"How early tomorrow?" Ty said.

"Someone opens seven A.M. It ain't me."

Ty laughed at the joke. Max didn't laugh. It wasn't a joke. The gunman was proud that he was important enough to not have to come in at seven A.M. Ty drove slowly out of the garage.

"You okay, Jupiter?"

"I'm fine. But I didn't see anything."

The garage doors closed behind them. Ty turned at the corner and pulled to the curb. Jupiter opened the passenger door, slid out and into the front seat.

"Did Tiburon come to the car wash?"

"Not until after five."

At the salvage yard they hurried into the trailer. Pete was counting his pay before putting it into the team's treasury. Calls to Bob's office and home failed to locate the elusive third Investigator, so they made their plans without him.

"I think we continue tomorrow exactly as we did

today," Jupiter said. "Pete goes to the car wash, Ty waits for a chance to sabotage Tiburon's car, and I watch in the garage."

"Tiburon better show up earlier tomorrow," Ty said, "or we're stymied."

◆   ◆   ◆

Tiburon did show up earlier the next day, but Ty had no chance to sabotage his graffiti-covered low-rider. Jupiter watched all day in the garage and saw nothing. The only good thing was that Tiburon liked Pete's energy and good humor—and the string tie with its shark head slide that hid Pete's mini walkie-talkie!

"You're a okay guy for an Anglo," Tiburon said. "That's a kick bolo slide, too. We find a big-bucks job for you, hey?"

Pete said he'd like that, but nothing more happened that day. Time was running out. Spring break would be over in three days.

But the next day Ty finally got his chance. Tiburon and the Piranhas came early and stopped at the Taco Bell. While they were all inside arguing about what to eat and how much, Ty slipped under Tiburon's low-rider and pulled two hidden wires from the electrical system. He had told Pete what he'd do. Pete would know just what to reconnect.

When Tiburon tried to start his car, nothing happened. As he worked at the car wash, Pete saw them all hovering and arguing around Tiburon's car. First the car-wash owner went over. Then one of the older employees. Finally, Tiburon yelled from the Taco Bell. "Hey, you, the new Anglo guy, come on over here!"

Pete dried his hands on a rag as he walked to the Taco Bell lot. "Me?"

"You're a hotshot mechanic, right? So let's see you get my heap running."

Pete leaned into the open hood. He looked at the engine, poked at the battery and spark plugs, and made noises. Then he slid under the car, where he knew the loose wires were but where no one else had thought to look.

"Someone hand me a half-inch combination wrench," Pete said from under the car.

There was a discussion about tools. The car-wash owner went to his office and returned with the proper wrench. Pete didn't need it, but it made him look much more impressive when he crawled out, saying, "Try it now."

The car started instantly.

"Hey, you sure know cars." Tiburon looked at Pete thoughtfully. "I'm gonna talk to some people could maybe use you. The pay's real, real good. I mean, *real* good. *Comprendes?*"

Tiburon was saying that the job was illegal, and asking Pete if he understood. Pete nodded.

◆   ◆   ◆

Jupiter was dozing in the Honda when he heard Ty's voice somewhere near the garage door.

"Just came to get something out of my car."

"Don't make it a habit. We don't like people coming here all day," Max's voice said.

Jupiter sank down out of sight.

"What's up?" Jupiter whispered.

Ty leaned in as if searching the car. "The trick worked! Tiburon told Pete someone'd come for him at the car wash and take him to a garage."

"When?"

"Today sometime. If this is where the chop shop is, they have to come past you."

After Ty had gone, Jupiter settled down to watch again. He was excited now. In the Honda, he was in a perfect position to see where they took Pete. Then he'd know where the chop shop was hidden.

An hour passed. Then two. Five o'clock came and went. At six, Jupiter heard Max lock the big double doors. Pete had not appeared. No one had. What if they'd been wrong all along, and the chop shop was somewhere else?

Jupiter's walkie-talkie suddenly gave a tiny beep. Jupe flicked it on. Ty's voice was low but urgent.

"Jupe! We've got trouble! Bad trouble!"

14

Wheels of Misfortune

"**I**'M LOCKED IN," JUPITER SAID INTO HIS WALKIE-talkie.

Ty's voice said, "Sneak out. Try the small door."

Jupiter tiptoed silently through the dimly lit garage to the door. The big doors were padlocked, but the small door just had a deadbolt. Twisting the knob on the lock, Jupe slipped out and saw the pickup at the corner.

"Get in," Ty said urgently.

"What is it?"

Ty was grim. "About fifteen minutes ago Bob drove like a maniac into the salvage yard with Pete's girl-friend, that Kelly Madigan. She said Pete told her what he was doing at the car wash and all about Tiburon and the stolen cars."

Jupiter groaned. "Pete tells her everything."

"Maybe it's good he does," Ty said. "Kelly just found out that another cheerleader, Tina Wallace, is El Tiburon's brand-new girlfriend! She's going around with him all the time—and she knows Pete, and who he is, and all about The Three Investigators!"

Jupiter was stunned. "If she spots Pete—"

"She could tell Tiburon all about him."

"And she could spot him anytime," Jupiter said.

"Kelly says Tina's a good kid and that she probably doesn't know anything about stolen cars. But there's no way of knowing when she might just stumble over Pete and say something."

They reached the salvage yard and the HQ trailer, where Bob and Kelly Madigan were waiting. The feisty, dark-haired cheerleader jumped up.

"Did you find him?" she demanded. "Did you get him away from there?"

"We don't even know where he is," Jupiter said. "You're sure he's left the car wash, Ty?"

"Tiburon came back and talked to him. Pete gave me thumbs up and drove off in the Fiero with Tiburon."

"Then," Bob said, "we've got to find him."

"But how?" Kelly asked, looking at each of them.

Bob and Ty looked at Jupiter. Kelly sat down, almost in tears.

"Jupiter?" she said. "Please?"

Jupiter stared at the wall as if he could see through it. He began to pinch his lower lip with his forefinger and thumb, a sure sign that he was deep in thought. "We must assume Pete was being taken to work in the chop shop. Therefore our problem is still the same—to locate the chop shop." Now he looked around at them.

"Not just if it's in that garage, but exactly where. In fact, we have to get inside it ourselves."

"Wait," Ty said. "We figure Pete's inside. And we figure the shop is in that garage. Can't we just contact him and he'll tell us where he is?"

"Yes!" Kelly cried, bouncing up again.

"No," Bob said. "We don't know for sure the shop's in that garage. And we can't risk contacting him on the walkie-talkies. We don't know who could be near him and hear."

"Bob's right," Jupiter said. "I think I have a plan, but it depends on Tiburon and the Piranhas being out of town tonight. Bob, can you find out—"

"They are!" Bob cut in, triumphant. "I can't believe our luck! I looked them up just out of curiosity. They're playing at a multiband outdoor gig up in Malibu."

"Chance favors the prepared mind," Jupiter pronounced. "You looked it up because all our years of detecting made you realize we might need to know."

"Whatever," Bob said. "Why do we need them out of town?"

"Because I'm gambling that the Mercedes wasn't the only car Tiburon swiped on his own and sent to the bodega," Jupiter said. "And other people besides the band seem to drop off cars at the bodega too. Torres gave a horn signal when he took that orange Caddy to the garage so they'd open the doors and let him in fast. Pete told me Torres gave the same signal with a second car. And I think what Ty was told to say at the bodega is a sort of password."

Ty watched Jupiter. "What have you got in mind, Jupe?"

"Tiburon's out of town. We get a car and drive it to the bodega. We turn it over to Torres. With any luck, he'll drive it to the chop shop!"

"How will that help Pete?" Kelly demanded.

"Two of us will be hidden in the car," Jupiter said. "I had the idea earlier, but it seemed too risky. Now we have to take the risk."

Bob asked the big question.

"Who hides in the car?"

"You're the only one Torres doesn't know," Jupiter said. "You'll have to drive the car. Ty and I will hide in the back."

"After I deliver it, then what do I do?" Bob wanted to know.

"Get in your own car and follow Torres."

"How do I get my car if I'm driving the stolen car?"

"Kelly drives it behind us and waits out of sight."

They each thought it over.

"Where do we get a car, Jupe?" Ty said. "Ours aren't worth stealing. You want us to really steal a car?"

Jupiter looked at Kelly. "I thought maybe Kelly could borrow her dad's Jaguar. That'd be worth stealing."

"Dad's Jag?" Kelly gulped. "Well, I mean, okay. If it'll get Pete out of there. Only you be careful with it."

"We will," Jupiter assured her. "Can you get it now?"

She nodded. "I guess."

"I'll take her," Bob said. "Show her how to drive my car on the way."

"When you get back," Jupiter said, "we'll set the details."

"Tiburon would need time to steal a car," Ty said.

Jupiter nodded. "We'll wait until midnight." He looked around at them. No one said anything more. "That's it, then. We go at midnight."

◆　　◆　　◆

It was five minutes before midnight when the elegant Jaguar glided up to the bodega. The store was still open.

Jupiter was in the trunk. Ty, the thinner of the two, was on the floor behind the front seat under a stadium blanket and some cushions. Bob wore a baseball cap and his old glasses. Kelly was behind them in Bob's VW, out of sight.

Joe Torres and his two henchmen, Nacio and Carlos, came out of the bodega and stared at the glistening Jaguar. Bob leaned out the window.

"Guy named Tiburon paid me a hundred dollars to drive his brother's car down from Malibu. You his brother?"

Torres nodded. "That's me. You delivered the car, you can take off now."

"I need a ride downtown."

"Call a cab," Torres said. "You got paid, now get lost."

Bob climbed out of the Jaguar and walked away into the night. In the trunk and under the blanket in the rear seat, Ty and Jupiter waited. They heard the footsteps of the three men approach the car.

"Hey, there's a blanket and cushions in back."

Joe Torres's voice laughed. "Some guy up in Malibu ain't just out a car, he's freezin', too!"

The front door opened on the driver's side.

"I'll take it over right now," Torres's voice said. "The shop's workin', and a Jag don't look right around here. At least Tib got this one delivered okay. Not two days late like last time."

The driver's door closed and the car started. It pulled away in a squeal of rubber and drove fast, with Jupiter hanging on in the trunk and Ty silent under the blanket.

◆   ◆   ◆

Bob jumped into his bug.

"Is everything okay?" Kelly asked, anxious.

"Torres bought it," Bob told her. "It looks like Jupe had it figured. Torres wasn't surprised at all. What I said seemed to be the right words."

Kelly pointed ahead. "There it goes! Dad's Jaguar!"

"Hang on," Bob said.

He turned the little red bug into the cross street behind the already distant Jaguar. The sleek import gave no sign of looking for or seeing a tail.

"Don't lose him, Bob!" Kelly pleaded.

"I'm doing the best I can," Bob said as he floored the gas pedal in pursuit of the Jaguar.

But the silver sedan moved steadily farther ahead as Bob tried desperately to keep up.

◆   ◆   ◆

In the trunk Jupiter held tight to keep from rolling and making noise as the Jaguar sped along. He was braced so tight that when the car suddenly screeched to a stop he almost slammed into the trunk wall. But he managed to make no noise. He heard Torres honk the signal: one long, two shorts, a long, and a short.

He heard a padlock being unlocked and heavy garage doors open. The Jaguar drove in.

"One of Tiburon's little extras," Torres's voice said.

"The boss ain't gonna be happy. That Mercedes got us into enough trouble."

It was the voice of Max the gunman!

The passenger door opened and someone got in. The car started again. In the dark, Jupiter sensed the Jag moving and turning slowly. Then it hesitated, bumped over something raised, and stopped.

There was a rattling sound. The slatted wooden gates of the car elevator were closing!

The elevator lurched upward.

Jupiter tried to gauge how far up it went, but he couldn't tell for sure.

The elevator stopped. Jupiter heard a faint rumbling sound.

The Jaguar started, then drove slowly off—in the wrong direction!

♦　　♦　　♦

"We've lost it, Bob!" Kelly wailed.

"It turned at that corner up there," Bob said grimly. "Maybe we can pick it up again."

Bob sped down the street in the commercial area, started to turn—and drove straight on past the cross street.

The Jaguar had been stopped in front of a three-story red-brick building a block up the street they just passed.

"You think he saw us?" Kelly asked.

"We're just another car. Torres never saw my bug."

Bob made a U-turn, drove back, and parked short of the corner. They ran to the corner and peered around. The Jaguar was gone. They moved along the dark and deserted street to the double doors where the Jag had gone in. There was a smaller door inside the large double doors.

Both doors were locked.

"What do we do?" Kelly whispered in despair.

"Hope that nobody shot the deadbolt home after Jupe left earlier," said Bob.

He reached into his jacket pocket and brought out a plastic ID card. He slid the card into the crack between the smaller door and its frame, next to the lock. After a moment, he managed to slip the latch. Seconds later they stood inside in the dimness of the Freeway Garage.

Bob and Kelly studied the rows and rows of parked cars.

"This must be where Jupe parked his Honda to watch," Bob said. "Look for your dad's Jag."

They moved through the vast, dim, silent room of parked cars. Finally they stood near the caged shaft of an automobile elevator. Its platform was somewhere above in the gloom. They listened for any sound, but heard nothing. No sounds, and no Jaguar.

"It's not here!" Kelly said, her voice rising.

"Shhhhh!" Bob hissed.

There was a sudden slamming noise, a rattle of wooden slats, and the car elevator began to descend!

"Quick!" Bob whispered.

He grabbed Kelly and dragged her behind the nearest row of cars. They crouched out of sight as the elevator reached the ground floor. Joe Torres stepped off alone and walked through the enormous room and out the front door.

Bob and Kelly stepped out to the elevator.

"My dad's car has to be somewhere up there," Kelly said, looking up the elevator shaft.

"Jupiter said he's sure the chop shop is hidden in the building," Bob agreed. "Only where is it?"

A voice spoke from behind them.

"It's a real shame you know about the chop shop, Andrews. You should have stuck to music."

Jake Hatch stood behind them, an ugly pistol in his thick hand. The burly man who stood on the other side of Bob and Kelly held an even bigger gun.

15

Walled In!

IN THE JAGUAR TRUNK JUPITER LISTENED. HE HEARD nothing. He had heard nothing for some time.

The Jaguar had seemed to drive straight through the wall at the rear of the elevator shaft. Then it had rolled to the right in an enclosed area, and stopped. Torres and the other man had walked away. After that there had been another faint rumbling noise, then silence.

Now, suddenly, clanging and hammering sounds sounded outside. Jupiter tapped on the trunk wall.

"Ty?"

Ty's voice came faintly through the wall. "You okay?"

"Yes. Where are we?"

"Let me look around."

Inside the trunk Jupiter waited.

"We're in what looks like another garage floor," Jupe finally heard Ty say. "It's not as big as the other floors. We're parked way off in a corner, but three guys are working on a Maserati across the room. One of them looks like Pete!"

"Get me out of here," Jupiter said.

He heard the faint sound of Ty moving, and then the key in the trunk lock. The lid lifted. Jupiter quickly rolled out, then crouched behind the sleek car with Ty.

Across the long, narrow room he saw three men working on what had once been a dark red Maserati. They were clearly taking it apart. They had almost everything off and spread around them. The chassis of the car sat like a skeleton with a bare engine block.

One of them *was* Pete.

"They put him to work pretty fast," Ty said in a low voice.

"Tiburon said he was okay, and they probably needed an extra man quickly," Jupiter said. "Look! He's still wearing his bolo tie. His walkie-talkie is in the clip. We can signal him. I don't think he's too close to the others."

The other two mechanics were working some distance from Pete. They talked low to each other and ignored their new co-worker. Both of them were short and skinny, with mean faces and sullen movements. Jupiter and Ty saw the butt of a pistol sticking out of the pocket of one of them.

"They're not paying any attention to Pete anyway," Ty said.

They were wrong. Jupiter activated the signal on his mini walkie-talkie. A small sound on Pete's device would alert him that they were nearby. Pete showed no reaction. He went on working. But one of the other mechanics looked up.

"What was that?"

Pete raised his head. "My digital watch alarm. There's a late-night show I like. I forgot to turn it off."

"What time is it anyway, kid?"

"Almost twelve thirty," Pete told them.

"Hey, let's speed this up, then. We got that Jag over there now, and Tiburon's gonna show with a bunch more anytime."

"Gosh," Pete said, "isn't it late to bring in cars?"

The other two laughed.

"Hey, the boss got to buy these lemon rejects when he got the chance, right?"

The two mechanics laughed harder. It was obvious to Jupiter and Ty that Pete had been told some big lie about what he was doing.

"Well," Pete said across the distance, "we're almost finished here. Maybe I should go and get the Jag."

"Sure, kid, go ahead."

Pete laid down his tools and wiped his hands on a rag. Then he walked to the Jaguar in the dark corner. He glanced back once to make sure that the other two were at work.

"Who's here?" he said, leaning into the Jaguar as if testing something. "Where's Kelly?"

He'd recognized the Jaguar, heard the signal, and put two and two together.

"Me and Ty," Jupiter said. "Kelly's with Bob. They

should be outside waiting. They were supposed to follow us. What's happening here?"

"It's a chop shop, all right," Pete said. "They gave me a phony story about the cars all having something really wrong with them. That makes them cheap buys and worth more as parts. But Tiburon made it pretty clear what's going on."

"Are both those guys armed?" Ty asked.

"Only one of them, I think."

"How come there's only two working, and you?" Ty asked.

Pete pretended to work on the Jag's front door. "Tiburon told me they were short because three mechanics were out sick. He laughed, so I think they're really in jail. I figure the rest of the gang, the real car thieves, are out stealing the cars. We got lucky, guys."

"Then let's get them now and call the police before anyone else shows up," Jupiter said.

Pete nodded and got into the front seat to drive the car. Jupiter and Ty slipped into the back and laid low. Pete started the car, driving it at a snail's pace toward the two mechanics at the Maserati.

Suddenly there was a rumbling nose. The left wall of the long room opened as if the bricks were all sliding sideways!

"It's a door!" Jupiter exclaimed softly. "In the rear wall of the elevator shaft! That's how they get the cars into the shop!"

The guys saw that the large section of wall was

made of fake bricks on a sliding door. It pushed in from the elevator side on steel hinges, then slid open sideways.

"We're in the building on the next street," Ty said. "And only half of it. It's a whole secret room hidden from both sides! The cars drive in as hot wheels and go out as parts."

"Guys!" Pete said, staring.

Jake Hatch and Max the gunman walked through the open wall out of the elevator. Bob and Kelly marched in front of them at gunpoint.

"He's got Kelly," Pete moaned. "We've got to rescue them, guys!"

Ty said, "We better jump them now, before any of the rest of the gang, or Tiburon and the Piranhas, show up."

"But they've got guns," Jupiter said in dismay.

Pete stopped the Jaguar, confused. What should they do? Jake Hatch and Max prodded Kelly and Bob toward the mechanics. Jake Hatch wore a grim expression.

"Caught them downstairs in the other building looking for a chop shop," he growled. "I guess they found one. Too bad they won't get to tell anyone about it."

"The other guys know where we are," Bob said, bluffing. "Ty'll bring the cops."

"That's the guy Tiburon got to drive that red Mercedes down from Oxnard," Max the gunman said.

"The one who brought the cops around to Torres."

"I told the bands not to steal cars on their own, the idiots," Hatch snarled.

"Tiburon only done it three times, Boss," Max said.

"That's three times too many." Jake Hatch shook his head. "Now we got to get rid of these two." He looked around. "Where's the new guy?"

"Over there getting the Jag," a mechanic said.

Pete said in a low voice, "They're going to spot us, guys. Hang on."

He drove the Jaguar slowly forward.

Hatch glanced toward the car. "Jag?"

"Yeah," the mechanic said. "Torres brought it half an hour ago. It's a 'present' from Tiburon."

"That jerk," Hatch said, shaking his head again. "Well, it looks like a good one, anyway." He turned back to Bob and Kelly. "Sorry about this, Andrews. You should've kept your nose out of my business."

Pete was getting closer. Hatch, Max the gunman, and the two mechanics stood in a group near the Maserati, facing Bob and Kelly. For a moment they had their backs to the Jaguar. Pete leaned out the window.

"Where do you want the Jag, Max?" he called out.

Jupiter and Ty saw the light glow in Bob's and Kelly's eyes as they recognized Pete's voice. In the backseat they tensed as Pete's foot eased down on the accelerator.

"What's that kid doing here?" Joe Torres stood in

the wide doorway of the elevator, pointing at Bob. "He's the kid who just drove that Jag in for—"

"Now, Pete!" Jupiter yelled.

Pete stomped hard on the gas pedal. The Jaguar leaped forward with a roar and a shriek of rubber straight toward the four men around the Maserati.

16

The Shark Sings

THE JAGUAR BORE DOWN ON THE FOUR MEN.

They stood frozen. They held their guns in a trance of terror, paralyzed by fear. Their horrified eyes stared at the car that rushed straight at them.

Then the instant broke, and they all dove wildly out of the car's deadly path. They sprawled on the littered floor, clawing for safety.

Max the gunman landed hard on his gun arm, cursed in pain, and lost the pistol.

The two mechanics scrambled over each other in their frantic dive out of the path of the hurtling Jaguar. The pistol popped out of the armed mechanic's pocket and skidded into the scattered parts of the dismantled Maserati.

Jake Hatch was the only one to keep his head. He rolled as he hit the floor, then came back up halfway with his pistol aimed straight at the Jaguar and Pete behind the wheel.

Bob pushed Kelly out of the path of the car and kicked the pistol out of Jake Hatch's hand with a *yoko-geri-keage* snap side kick. The pistol skidded part-way across the room. Hatch lunged at Bob, who countered instantly with an elbow strike to the head that sent Jake sprawling.

The Jaguar screamed to a stop inches from the dismantled Maserati.

Pete flung himself out of the car and leaped on Jake Hatch as the chop-shop boss tried to get up once more.

Ty was out and running at Joe Torres, who still stood near the open wall, apart from the others, trying to pull his pistol from his pocket. The two went down in a flurry of arms and legs as Ty made a flying tackle on the bodega owner.

Jupiter ran toward Bob, who was battling Max. The powerful thug was back on his feet, lunging toward his pistol. Bob tried to reach the compact gunman with a *tobi-yoko-geri* jumping side kick, but Max held him off with a sweeping back arm block of his own. He bent to grab at his gun.

Jupiter slammed into the bent-over gunman, sending him down again. Swearing, Max bounced up and charged. This time Jupiter felled him with a hip throw, then dove on top of him. Bob piled on top of Jupe. The angry gunman cursed and swore but stayed down under the weight of both of them.

Untangled, the two mechanics started to get up, then stopped. They stared into the angry eyes and steady hands of Kelly Madigan. The cheerleader had picked up Jake Hatch's big pistol. She held it now in both her small hands, aiming it at the two suddenly frozen mechanics.

"Easy, little lady."

"We ain't gonna move, girl. You just hold that thing easy."

The two held out their hands toward Kelly as if to ward off the bullets her nervous trigger finger might let loose. It was obvious they weren't even going to try to get up.

"That's good thinking, guys," Kelly said, waving the gun a little. "You just sit right there."

Pete chopped Jake Hatch with a sharp *nukite* sword hand strike to the solar plexus, which knocked all the wind out of the boss of the gang. Hatch lay on the littered floor and groaned, holding his chest.

Ty knocked the out-of-shape Torres out cold, took his gun, and put it into his belt. He crossed the room to Kelly and took the gun from her hands.

Bob and Jupiter found a length of wire and tied Max's hands and ankles. He lay swearing and struggling, but helpless.

Grinning, Bob stood up. "Well, I guess that takes care of the stolen-car gang."

"We've got them!" Pete cried.

"And the evidence," Jupiter added, nodding at the stripped Maserati.

"Better tie them all and pick up the guns," Ty said. "I'll hold this gun on them."

Pete and Jupiter found some rope in a corner, then tied up the two mechanics and Torres. Bob retrieved the mechanic's gun from among the car parts and picked up Max's pistol from the floor. Pete and Jupiter turned to tie up Jake Hatch. He was still groaning and holding his bruised ribs as if he'd never recover.

But before they could take care of the agent, they heard feet pounding, and a gang of men poured into the room from an alcove beyond the Maserati.

"Hey, we got six nice hot wheels waitin' for the elevator down on the first floor," El Tiburon said as he strode in through some door the guys hadn't seen. He stopped and stared. "*Ay chihuahua!* Look at this, hey?"

The four Piranhas and some hangers-on stood behind the handsome Latino bandleader, who still wore his white stage suit.

Jupiter stepped out to face them. "It's over, Tiburon. We've got your boss, his gunmen, Joe Torres, and the stolen car. You all better give yourselves up."

"Yeah?" Tiburon said. He looked around. He looked at the guns in Ty's and Bob's hands. He looked at the four Piranhas and the others behind him. Then he said to Jupe, "Hey, man, I don't know, you know? I mean, there's a lot more of us, right?"

Jake Hatch sat up on the floor, suddenly recovered. "Take care of these kids, Tiburon! Jump them!"

Tiburon shrugged. "I don' know, bossman. They got guns, you know? You guys ain't gonna be a lotta help."

"They're just stupid kids! They don't even know how to use the guns. You can take them."

"Maybe, hey?" the smiling Latino said. "But I been

figuring it's maybe time me and the band was getting raises, you know?"

"I pay you too much now!" Hatch raged. "Get these kids. You and your dumb extra cars got us into this, you stupid *pachuco!*"

Tiburon stared at Hatch. Behind him the Piranhas muttered angrily. Tiburon seemed to listen to the rumble of anger in their voices.

Jupiter saw the change. He moved quickly and talked straight to Tiburon.

"He's been using you, Tiburon. Using all of you. He hasn't any respect for you. You and the Piranhas are just useful jerks to him."

Tiburon didn't appear to hear Jupiter. He was too busy staring at Jake Hatch. "Hey, you want help from a gang of dumb *pachucos*, bossman? Hey, you don' know one from the other, right? They all look the same, them dumb *pachucos*, right?"

Hatch turned purple where he sat on the floor. "Get us out of here or you're finished, you hear! Take care of these kids, you brainless *cholo*, or you'll never work for me again, you hear?"

Tiburon shook his head. "Hey, what can a bunch of dumb *pachucos* do? *Cholos estúpidos?* Hey, they're all lazy an' greasy, right? Fat greasers." He smiled at Hatch, then looked at Jupiter. "Hey, fat Anglo, we tell you all about this smart bossman an' his big-time operation. You tell the cops they should go nice an' easy on Tiburon and the Piranhas, okay?"

"You know we can't tell the cops what to do,

Tiburon," Ty said, still holding Hatch's gun and watching the Piranhas.

"But we'll do everything we can," Jupiter added quickly. "We know you mostly only delivered the cars here. Other guys stole them for Hatch, professional crooks. The gang's mechanics chopped them up, not you guys."

Tiburon nodded. "You pretty smart for a young guy. Yeah, they give us the cars all painted up to look like our regular wheels, and we drive 'em to the gigs an' back here. Or maybe they take us to the gig, and we only drive 'em back."

"What about that red Mercedes?" Ty asked grimly. "The one you stole in Oxnard."

Tiburon shrugged. "Okay, so I steal a couple cars myself when they don't got no cars ready for us. It was dumb. I louse it up anyway."

Jupiter said, "If you turn state's evidence and testify in court against Hatch and his gang, the judge will give you a break for sure."

"Don't listen to them!" Jake Hatch cried, pulling away from Pete and lunging toward Tiburon. "I'll give you a raise. All of you. You'll be the richest wetbacks in town."

Tiburon looked at Hatch, at Jupiter and Ty, then at the Piranhas behind him. He shrugged.

"Okay, smart Anglo, let's go talk to the cops."

Ty lowered his gun. Pete grinned. Bob and Jupiter breathed more easily. Kelly ran to Pete and threw her arms around him. Pete blushed bright red. Kelly laughed, kissed Pete, and stepped back.

Jake Hatch suddenly jumped and grabbed Kelly. He held her in front of him, twisted her arm behind her, and backed toward the elevator. Anybody who tried to shoot him would hit the girl.

"Everyone stay right where they are! Anyone comes near me, this little lady gets hurt. You got that?"

No one moved as Hatch backed into the elevator with his hostage. The wall slowly closed on him and the terrified Kelly.

17

The Hottest Wheels

IN THE CHOP SHOP THERE WAS A SHOCKED SILENCE. Pete ran to the closed wall.

"How do you open this? Quick!"

He stared at Tiburon, who shrugged. "I don' know, man. Someone always open it for us."

Joe Torres laughed. "Figure it out yourself, hotshot."

"The boss is too smart for you punks," Max the gunman sneered.

The two mechanics shook their heads. They didn't know how to open the hidden door. Jupiter whirled to face Tiburon.

"How did you get in here?"

"The office over there," Tiburon said. "Same way we always go out."

"Office? Where?" Pete said. "Show me. Hurry!"

"Sure, man, only the stairs down come out on the wrong street, you know? I mean, you gotta go all around to the front to get in the garage."

"Show me!" Pete cried.

"I'll go with you," Ty said, tucking one pistol into his belt and handing the other one to Bob. "They're tied up good, but keep an eye on them."

Tiburon took Ty and Pete to the alcove in the far corner of the room, opposite the wall with the elevator. The door to the office was out of sight around the alcove's corner.

"You gotta know the trick," Tiburon said. He pulled a small fire extinguisher on the wall. The office door opened.

Pete and Ty raced through a small business office and down the stairs into the night. A moon had come up, lighting their way in silvery blue. They ran around the building, past Pete's Fiero parked on the side street, to the front of the garage.

The double doors were still closed and locked!

"He's got to be inside!" Pete said.

"Unless there's another way out we don't know," Ty said. "Be careful, Pete. He's got Kelly."

Pete nodded. He tried the small door. It was unlocked. They stepped through into the parking floor. Only one night light was lit, far to the rear, near the elevator.

They listened in the darkness.

There was no sound.

"He's gone," Pete moaned in despair. "And Kelly's with him."

Ty listened. "I'm not so sure. Hear that?"

Pete heard the small tapping sound. Like something light hitting metal. It seemed to come from the rear of the room to the right of the elevator.

"It's a fingernail hitting a car!" Pete said. "It's Kelly. Come on."

He hurried among the cars with Ty close behind. They came out in the rear at the open aisle near the elevator. They stood in the aisle and listened.

Car lights suddenly blazed on their right.

Lights aimed directly at them along the cross aisle where they stood!

A car at the far end of the aisle roared into life. There was a scream of tires as it shot toward them, gaining speed at every foot.

They jumped back out of the aisle as the silver car slammed past and screamed to a halt, smashing into parked cars at the far end of the aisle.

"It's a Rolls-Royce!" Pete exclaimed.

He had no time to say anything more. The Rolls backed, turned, screamed in a circle, smashing more cars, and thundered back toward them.

"He's going to try to crush us between cars," Ty cried. "Jump!"

They scrambled again as the Rolls slammed into the car they had been hiding behind, crushing it into the next one and the next.

They ran.

But wherever they ran the Rolls-Royce pursued them, crashing into cars, slamming cars into each other, tearing off fenders and bumpers.

Ty pulled Hatch's pistol from his belt and tried to get a clear shot at the charging Rolls as it pursued them around the dark garage.

"Kelly's in there!" Pete yelled. "Don't shoot!"

"I'll try for the tires," Ty cried, and sprawled again out of the path of the relentless Rolls.

It was turning into a wreck itself, but the powerful handmade car kept moving. It was far too strong to be as badly damaged as the cars it hit.

Suddenly Ty saw a clear shot at its tires. He fired twice.

"Missed!" Ty groaned.

The Rolls lurched off and sideswiped four more cars, slamming them into one another in a tangle of torn metal.

This time it did not try to follow the guys. Instead, it moved toward one of the cross aisles.

"He's going to get out!" Pete shouted.

"It's the gun!" Ty cried. "He won't risk the gun."

The Rolls raced down the cross aisle that led to the main front aisle. Ty and Pete pounded through the mangled cars to cut it off.

"He's got to get out to unlock the doors!" Pete shouted. "We've got him!"

They had almost reached the double doors when the Rolls squealed in a sharp left turn and came down the exit aisle at full speed.

"He's not going to stop!" Ty yelled.

At high speed, yet almost in slow motion, the great

silver car smashed straight through the heavy wooden doors.

"Back to my car!" Pete cried. "Hurry!"

"No time," Ty said, panting. "He's going to get away."

Pete didn't answer. He ran through the smashed doors.

The silver Rolls, going too fast, had failed to make the full turn into the street. It had skidded into the fence on the other side and was backing and turning to drive away. Pete ran along the street and around the corner to his Fiero.

"He's got too much head start, Pete," Ty cried as they tumbled into the Fiero.

But as they rounded the corner the Rolls was still there! It swayed and wobbled and jerked along the street like an injured duck.

"It's damaged." Ty grinned. "We—"

"No, look!" Pete cried.

Inside the car, shadows struggled.

"Kelly's fighting him. Trying to stop him."

Even as Pete spoke, the passenger door of the Rolls flew open and Kelly sprawled onto the street.

The Rolls-Royce raced away.

Kelly jumped up right in the path of the Fiero. Pete skidded to a stop. He leaned out.

"We'll catch him, Kelly!"

Kelly pulled the passenger door open and tumbled over Ty into the narrow backseat.

"Not without me you don't," she snapped, and smiled breathlessly at them.

Pete grinned at her.

"Hang on, then," he said. "This is going to be a dynamite ride."

Pete caught up with the battered Rolls in less than three blocks. Even Ty was pale as Pete drove like a madman, following the great silver machine through every twist and turn it tried to make.

Together the two cars raced through the dark streets.

The Rolls plunged across a vacant lot, dodged among the pillars under the freeway, drove down the railroad tracks. It couldn't shake Pete. It turned the wrong way up one-way streets, tried to outrun them on the straight beachfront boulevard.

There was no escape from Pete's determination.

Finally Hatch made a last desperate attempt to reach the freeway. The entrance was a sharp left turn under an overhead bridge. For one instant it seemed that the fleeing chop shop operator would make it.

Then Pete cut the Fiero in front of the Rolls as it slowed for the final sharp turn into the entrance. Hatch swerved around the Fiero, hung on the edge of the entrance, skidded sideways into the massive concrete freeway support, and came to a steaming, shuddering stop.

Ty was out of the Fiero in an instant. He ripped open the Rolls-Royce's door and dragged Jake Hatch out by the collar. He hustled the dazed Hatch into the backseat of the Fiero and sat on him.

"I guess Hatch knows now who's got the hottest wheels," Ty said.

Kelly looked admiringly at Pete. He grinned at Ty and drove back to the garage.

When they arrived, everyone was out front. Tiburon and the Piranhas stood off to the right, waiting. The prisoners were guarded by Bob. Pete added the still dazed Jack Hatch to the prisoners.

"Anyone call the police?" Ty asked.

Bob nodded. "Jupe said he was going to."

Pete looked around. "Hey, where is Jupe?"

A terrible moan came from inside the garage. Jupiter stood among the litter of smashed cars. He was staring at the demolished remains of something they couldn't recognize. Then Bob guessed what it was.

"It's your new Honda?"

The little blue and white car was a total wreck! Hatch had smashed into it again and again.

"No wheels." Jupiter groaned. "And now I'm broke, too!"

The others comforted their despairing leader as best they could. Ty promised he'd help Jupe get an even better car.

"There'll be some insurance money," Ty said. "And we'll think of something to make extra cash." He smiled. "Hey, did you call the cops, Jupe?"

Jupiter sighed. "When I saw my car, I forgot."

Then he managed a weak smile. "Well, at least we got the chop-shop ring, and cleared you, Ty!"

Police cars suddenly appeared at both ends of the street. Officers jumped out with guns drawn and ran toward the guys and their prisoners. In the lead were Detective Cole and Sergeant Maxim.

"Hey," Ty said. "That Sergeant Maxim thinks he finally caught me red-handed, guys!"

And with a big grin, Ty raised his hands in mock surrender.

The Three Investigators just laughed.

Murder to Go

1

Smashing Beauty

PETE CRENSHAW ZIPPED HIS CAR INTO THE OUTDOOR parking lot of Rocky Beach Memorial Hospital and hit the brakes. He revved the engine of the used '81 Scirocco a couple of times, loud and hard, then switched off the ignition. The windshield wipers stopped in the middle of their arc.

Pete liked to think he was just like his car—lean, mean, and prone to quick moves. At over six feet tall and built like a decathlon athlete, he wasn't far wrong.

"Wow. This is serious rain. And I mean *serious*," Pete said to his friend Jupiter Jones, who was sitting next to him.

Jupiter Jones was neither lean nor mean. He preferred to describe himself as "well padded" or "husky." He never seemed to run out of substitutes for "overweight." Most people would have laughed at Jupe's attempts to disguise the truth. But Pete kept the teasing to a minimum. After all, seventeen-year-old Jupiter was Pete's best friend. And Jupe was also the founder

149

of The Three Investigators. Along with Bob Andrews, they were Rocky Beach, California's most famous detectives.

The two of them sat in the car and watched the storm. It was more than the typical summer downpour. Rain pounded the windshield. Then, just when Pete and Jupe were least expecting it, lightning flashed and crashed.

"Come on. It's never going to let up," Pete said, brushing his reddish-brown hair out of his eyes. "And visiting hours are almost over. Kelly's waiting for me."

"You can't let girls boss you around," Jupe said, unbuckling his seat belt reluctantly.

"I hate to tell you this," Pete said to Jupe, "but girls are the one subject you're not an expert on."

"True," Jupe admitted. "However, as you well know, that won't stop me from giving you advice."

Pete laughed.

Then the two friends pulled up the hoods of their Windbreakers and made a dash through the rain for the hospital entrance.

Inside the hospital lobby they shook out their wet jackets and hurried to room 2113.

When they got there, Kelly Madigan was lying in her hospital bed, talking on the phone and twirling a curl of her long brown hair with her fingers. The TV was on, playing music videos with the sound off. She didn't look like someone who had just had her appendix taken out three days ago.

Kelly was a pretty, energetic cheerleader at Rocky

Beach High School, the same school Pete, Jupe, and Bob attended. One day six months ago she suddenly decided that Pete Crenshaw ought to be going steady and he ought to be going steady with her. Pete didn't put up much of a fight.

"Gotta hang up, Sue," Kelly said, giving Pete and Jupe a small wave. "Time for my Friday night date. My own personal hunk just walked in with a friend." Then Kelly laughed. "Is the friend a hunk too?" Kelly said, repeating what Sue had just asked her. She looked Jupe up and down with her large green eyes.

Jupe tried to stare back at her but then he got nervous and looked away.

"Depends, Sue," Kelly said. "Do you think Frosty the Snowman's a hunk?" she added with a teasing but sweet laugh.

Jupe crossed his arms and sat down grumpily on one of the uncomfortable wooden chairs that were standard in hospital rooms.

Suddenly Kelly held out the phone—to Jupe! "Sue wants to talk to you," she said, smiling.

Jupe swallowed hard and tried to look as though he didn't know the meaning of the word "panic." Talking to suspects in a mystery was no problem. Talking to girls—that was Bob Andrews' department.

"Go on, Jupe," Pete teased. He was sitting on the bed next to Kelly.

Jupe slowly stood up and took the phone.

"Hello," he said formally, "this is Jupiter Jones speaking." Jupe paused.

"Hi," said a girl's voice with a nervous giggle. "I'm Sue. How's it going?"

"How is what going?" Jupe asked. His logical mind required logical questions before he could give a logical answer.

"Oh, I don't know, you know," said Sue.

Jupe cleared his throat and squinted one eye at Kelly. He wished he didn't have an audience for this phone call. Pete and Kelly were holding hands and grinning at him.

"Don't you want to know if I'm cute or something?" Sue asked on the other end of the line.

Just then a nurse with bright copper-red hair stuck her head in the door. "Visiting hours are over. You'll have to leave now," she said.

Jupe sighed with relief and handed the phone back to Kelly. "I'll call you later," Kelly told Sue, hanging up quickly. Then she winked at Jupe. "Jupiter Jones, ladies' man, strikes again," she said.

Suddenly the door banged open. A doctor, two orderlies, and two nurses pushed a gurney into the room at top speed. Jupe had to jump out of the way.

They had a patient on the gurney, a young woman with dark curly hair. Her pretty face was pale, bruised, and bandaged. She was unconscious.

"New roommate for you, Kelly," said the doctor, a young intern with a short ponytail and a calm smile. He helped lift the new patient onto the second bed in Kelly's green hospital room.

"Is she hurt badly?" Kelly asked.

"Her wounds appear superficial," Jupe said. His eyes never missed anything. "My guess is she's just recovering from a concussion and mild shock."

"Hey—great diagnosis," the doctor said, looking over at Jupe with a surprised smile.

The hospital team gently settled the young woman into the bed and then hooked up her i.v., which started the medication dripping. When they were certain she was secure, the nurses and orderlies backed away and the doctor wrote notes on her chart.

"What happened to her?" Kelly asked the doctor in a concerned voice.

"Car smash-up on Countyline Drive. She went right off the road. We always get a couple on a rotten night like this," he said, moving toward the door to leave. "She's a celebrity's kid, although it's hard to tell with all the bumps and bruises. She's—"

But before the doctor could finish his sentence, the nurse with the copper-red hair opened the door again. "I said it once. I'll say it again," she barked at Jupe and Pete. "Hospital visiting hours are over. This means you must leave immediately. The only exception is if you are very sick, in which case please see the admissions nurse."

"We get the message," Pete said.

"Good," said the nurse with a pinched smile. "I guess I won't have to call out the guard dogs tonight."

As she turned and left the room, Pete leaned down and gave Kelly a quick kiss. "See you tomorrow, babe. I'm staying at Jupe's tonight."

Jupe, however, was looking at the new patient's chart.

"Hey—what are you doing?" Pete asked.

"Just satisfying my curiosity," Jupe answered. "The doctor left before telling us who she is. Who's Juliet Coop?"

Pete looked at Jupe and shrugged. The name didn't set off any bells. So they said good-bye to Kelly and left.

But a minute later both Pete and Jupe knew exactly who Juliet Coop was, because as they headed toward the elevator a huge man came rushing out of it and went straight to the nurses' station. He leaned over the desk so that his worried face was close to the nurse with the copper-colored hair. "Where's my daughter?" he asked. "Where is she?"

"That's Big Barney Coop!" Jupe said, recognizing the man instantly.

"Right. The Chicken King!" Pete exclaimed.

It had to be. He was wearing the familiar red, white, and blue jogging suit, just like the one he wore on TV. And everyone in Southern California knew Big Barney Coop's face. You couldn't flip the TV channels without seeing him in a commercial for Chicken Coop fast-food restaurants.

"Juliet Coop—Barney Coop," said Jupe. "She must be the Chicken King's daughter."

"Room 2113, Mr. Coop," said the nurse.

"Is that a lucky room?" asked Big Barney. "I want

my daughter in a lucky room. Where is it? Which way? Which room?"

Jupiter felt sorry seeing Big Barney so upset and disoriented. He walked over to the nurse's desk. "Mr. Coop, it's that room," Jupe said, pointing.

Big Barney Coop, who was practically a foot taller than Jupe, looked down. "You sure?" he asked.

"My friend and I were visiting the patient who's sharing your daughter's room," Jupe said. "As a matter of fact, Juliet is sleeping now."

That seemed to be enough reassurance to make the Chicken King relax a little. "Here are a couple of freebies," he said, handing Jupe two coupons from his sweatshirt pocket. "I like you, guy. Plump but tender. I'll bet you'd look great dipped in my secret golden batter. Thanks, guy."

Jupe smiled and watched Big Barney walk into the hospital room. Then he tore up the coupons.

"Hey!" Pete said, grabbing for the coupons, but too late. "Why'd you do that, Jupe?"

"My diet," Jupe said unhappily. "No fried foods allowed, remember?"

"Yeah, I remember," Pete said. "And you have to eat a piece of melon with every meal. Weird. But just because *you're* dieting doesn't mean *I* am. I *love* the Chicken Coop's fried chicken."

"Don't even talk about it," Jupe moaned. "I love it too. I can smell that crispy crust and juicy tender white meat right now."

They dashed out into the rain-soaked parking lot and Pete drove them back toward Jupe's house. Jupe lived with his Aunt Mathilda and Uncle Titus Jones, who owned a junkyard across the street. When Jupe, Pete, and Bob were kids, they hung around the junkyard together, especially when they were on a case. The Three Investigators even had their secret headquarters there, in a trailer that was hidden by junk. But now that they were seventeen years old, the trailer was no longer hidden, and they mostly hung around in Jupe's electronics workshop, which was right next door.

"Too bad we couldn't have heard the details of Juliet Coop's car crash," Jupe said. Then he noticed Pete looking at him out of the corner of his eye. "I know, I know. There's no sign of anything mysterious about it. I just have this feeling. Call it a premonition."

Finally Pete pulled into the junkyard and they splashed through the mud into Jupe's workshop. Inside were desks and countertops filled with high-tech electronic gadgets and parts, catalogs of modern surveillance equipment, tools, high school notebooks, empty pizza boxes, music tapes, and a couple of chairs. There was also an answering machine, and as always Jupe checked it first thing.

"Hi, guys," said a familiar voice on the message tape. It was Bob Andrews, the third Investigator. "Sorry I didn't make it over to the hospital tonight to see Kelly. I had to check out a new band for the agency because the boss is out of town. Then Jennifer called to remind me that we had a date, which came as a shock to me and an even bigger shock to Amy, who I was supposed to meet for a clambake on the beach. Guess those clams got rained out. Anyway, Jupe, maybe you can work out a data base computer program for me, to prevent accidents like this from happening. Think about it. Talk to you guys tomorrow."

"Bob works too hard at that talent agency." Jupe scowled as he turned off the answering machine.

"I know," Pete said with a smile. "All that work cuts into his dating time."

Jupe started tinkering with a small device that was supposed to read electronic lock combinations, and Pete busied himself at another table, cleaning out the sprayer of a new fuel injector for his car. They talked until it got very late.

They talked about Jupe's wish for a car, about not seeing Bob too much anymore because of his job, and about running into Big Barney Coop. And Jupe talked about Juliet Coop's accident. It drove him crazy not to know the details about something.

Suddenly the telephone rang, startling both Pete and Jupe. They looked at the clock. Nearly midnight. Pretty late for calls, even on a Friday night.

Jupe sat down in an old swivel chair. It had a Niagara Falls 1982 souvenir pillow for its cushion. "The Three Investigators," he said in an I-mean-business voice.

"Jupe, it's Kelly. Put me on the speaker phone, okay? I've got to talk to both of you."

"It's Kelly," Jupe said as he switched on the speaker phone.

Pete looked as surprised as Jupe. "What's going on, Kel?" Pete asked.

"Something weird," Kelly said. "Juliet Coop has been moaning and talking in her sleep."

Jupe got that feeling again. But he didn't want to jump to conclusions. "Bad dreams aren't uncommon after an accident like hers," Jupe said.

"Okay, okay," Kelly said impatiently. "But it's *what* she's dreaming about that freaks me. She keeps saying, 'Millions of people will die.' "

The words gave Jupe and Pete a chill.

"And that's not all," Kelly continued. "She keeps saying, 'He's poisoning the chicken. It's wrong. It's wrong.' And she sounds like she means it. I mean, it doesn't sound like a dream."

Pete let out a low whistle. "Heavy duty."

"I *told* you I had a feeling!" Jupe said.

"Yeah," said Pete. "But who knew it meant the Chicken King was poisoning my favorite food!"

2

After-hours Visitors

"HELLO?" KELLY MADIGAN'S PUZZLED VOICE CAME out of the speaker phone in Jupe's workshop. "Are you guys still there?"

They were there, but their tongues were in shock. How many times had they eaten at a Chicken Coop restaurant in their lives? Hundreds? Thousands? Probably more for Jupe. How many times had they seen Big Barney Coop's friendly face on TV and heard his crazy but sincere voice telling them, "I've built my reputation selling legs and not pulling yours."

"Big Barney Coop . . . poisoning his food . . . ?" Pete said, shaking his head. His voice trailed off and his face got serious. "I can't believe it."

"And there's no reason why we should," Jupe said, having given the matter some thought. "As Aunt Mathilda frequently reminds me, the trouble with jumping to conclusions is you don't know what you're going to land in."

"What's that mean?" Pete said.

"It means," said Jupe, "we can't accuse Big Barney

159

Coop of *anything*. For one thing, there's no reason to think that Big Barney is the person Juliet was talking about in her sleep. It could be anyone who's poisoning the chicken. And for all we know, Juliet Coop is having a bad reaction to her medication or to the shock of her accident, or maybe she's just having bad dreams."

"Hey, guys," Kelly said, talking into her hospital phone. "I'd love to put Juliet on the line so you could talk to her personally, but the phone cord's not long enough to reach her in dreamland. Oh, listen . . . did you hear that?"

Pete shook his head. Jupe answered out loud, since Kelly couldn't see through the telephone. "No. What?" Jupe asked.

"She said it again," Kelly reported. "She said, 'No—people will die. Don't do it!' "

"Okay," Jupe said to Kelly. "We'll be there at eleven A.M. tomorrow to talk to Juliet. That's when visiting hours start. I'm certain she can tell us whether this was just a bad dream or not."

"Fine," Kelly said. "But I'm telling you there's a mystery here."

"See you in the morning, babe," Pete said, and hung up the phone.

Nobody got much sleep that night. For one thing, Jupe stayed up trying to figure out who would want to poison millions of people, and why. Was it Big Barney? Or was Juliet Coop mixed up with some kind of crazy political terrorist group? Or was there someone else who would want to poison the Chicken Coop's prime fillets?

Then at two in the morning Jupe called Bob Andrews to fill him in and to make sure he'd be at the hospital early too.

After the phone call, Bob had trouble falling back to sleep because he knew that when Jupe got into one of his agitated moods, he called frequently.

Kelly didn't sleep, either. She stayed awake in her hospital bed most of the night, waiting for Juliet Coop to say something more. Every time Juliet moaned in her bed, Kelly would ask her softly, "Who, Juliet? Who's poisoning the chicken?" But Juliet didn't answer.

Pete slept like a rock.

The next day bright sunlight filled Kelly's hospital room when Pete and Jupe arrived.

The first thing Jupe noticed—besides the fact that Kelly looked very tired, and that the number of vases of flowers in the room had quadrupled during the night, and that a large stuffed chicken wearing a golden crown now occupied the guest chair by Juliet's bed—was that the curtains had been drawn around Juliet Coop, sealing her off.

"Who's in there?" Jupe asked, pointing to the curtained area. He wanted to talk to Juliet right away and settle this mystery.

"Shhh." Kelly hushed Jupe and then spoke in a whisper. "No one's in there except Juliet. I think she's asleep."

Just then Bob Andrews walked in.

"Sorry I'm late guys. Car trouble," the tall, lanky teen said, taking off the cotton sweater that was tied around his neck.

Bob had always been a thin kid with glasses who was good at school but usually got lost in the background. Maybe it was because he worked for so many years in the dark, hidden stacks of the town library.

But all of that was changed now. Contact lenses, brighter clothes, a job with Sax Sendler's talent agency, a car of his own, karate lessons, and a lot of self-confidence had transformed The Three Investigators' researcher into one of the most popular guys at Rocky Beach High School.

"Where's our case? Or did the Chicken Princess fly the coop?" Bob asked.

"The case is behind the curtains," Pete said, motioning with a jerk of his head. "She's asleep. We can't talk to her."

"I'm sure that Jupe would be the first to point out that logically we *could* talk to her all we wanted," Bob said with a smile. "She just won't answer."

"At least she's quiet now," Kelly said softly. "You should have heard her moaning all night. And she had some interesting visitors."

"In the middle of the night?" Jupe said, surprised. "How'd they get past the nurse with the red hair and hot temper?"

Kelly shrugged. "Very mysterious, isn't it?"

"Who were they?" Jupe asked skeptically.

"Well, Big Barney was in here every hour. He even gave me a couple of free coupons," Kelly said.

"Who else?" asked Jupe.

"A good-looking guy named Sean Fellows," Kelly said.

"How do you know his name?" Pete asked, suddenly frowning.

"Because I asked him—and don't be so jealous," Kelly said. "He's Juliet's ex-boyfriend. He came at about four A.M. and just sat there watching her. Then early this morning there was another visitor, Maria Gonzales. She said she was Juliet's college roommate."

"We can forget about her," Jupe said.

"Why?" Bob asked.

"Because Juliet said, 'He's poisoning the chicken,' " Jupe explained. "And I'm not too worried about this Sean Fellows, either. An ex-boyfriend doesn't sound like someone who would kill millions."

"Not even for revenge?" Pete asked.

Jupe gave a "maybe" shrug.

"But you haven't heard about mystery guest number four," Kelly said, lowering her voice even more.

The four teenagers looked toward the closed curtains around Juliet's bed to be sure she wasn't waking up. Then Kelly continued her story. "The fourth person I call Mr. Sweetness," she said. "He was like a brick wall with a bad temper. He was big, in his thirties, wearing an army camouflage jacket. As soon as he saw me, he put the collar up to hide his face. Maybe 'cause he was so ugly!"

"Why didn't you ask *his* name?" said Pete grumpily.

"Hey—I *did*, and he told me to mind my own business. And he meant it," Kelly said. "Then he drew the curtains around Juliet's bed so I couldn't see anything."

"But what did you *hear*?" asked Jupe.

"Well," Kelly said, "I heard him go through her closet and after that, every drawer on her side of the room."

"Slowly or quickly?" Jupe asked.

"Quickly," Kelly answered with a decisive nod.

Jupe smiled. "From that I'd have to conclude that he wasn't just browsing. He knew exactly what he was looking for."

"But he didn't find it. He left empty-handed," Kelly added.

"Unfortunately, there's no way to get any more answers until Juliet wakes up," Jupe said, starting to pace the floor.

"And she'd better wake up during visiting hours or the dragon lady will kick us out again," Pete said.

Bob peeked around the corner of Juliet's curtains. "She doesn't look too bad," he said. "The newspaper this morning said she was lucky to be alive. She totaled her car in the crash." Bob turned back to his friends. "Have you been to the scene of the accident yet?"

Jupe shook his head and kept pacing back and forth. Just then the nurse with red hair came into the room carrying a large bouquet of flowers.

She looked at Kelly and then at each of the guys in the room. "Three boys?" she said, shaking her head at Kelly. "Don't you think you should let someone else have one?" She set the flowers down by Juliet's bed and then walked to the door. "I'll be back," she said, almost like a warning.

"What for?" Pete muttered when she was gone.

"Well, this is interesting," Bob said, examining the flowers the nurse had left. "These are from Michael Argenti."

"Why is that interesting?" asked Pete.

"Because he's the competition," Bob said. "He owns the Roast Roost restaurants."

"How do you know all this stuff? I mean, between you and Jupe, it's disgusting," Pete said.

Bob laughed. "No, it's just that one of the bands we handle at the agency just played at the grand opening of a new Roast Roost franchise. And Michael Argenti was supposed to be there, but he kept us waiting four hours in the hot sun until he showed up."

"Can you explain why Argenti would send flowers to the daughter of his rival?" asked Jupe.

"Sax does things like that sometimes," said Bob. "It's a business practice. Doesn't mean you actually like the guy. I heard Argenti and Big Barney can't stand each other. Every time Michael Argenti makes a wish on a wishbone, he wishes Big Barney would drop dead. And it's the same for Big Barney."

"Well, now at least we've got some suspects," Pete said, pounding his fist into his hand.

"Yeah, but do we have a crime?" Jupe asked.

At that moment Big Barney Coop opened the door. He froze for a second, obviously surprised at seeing a roomful of people.

Jupe studied Big Barney's full, round face. What was that deep in his eyes? Was it the look of a father worried for his daughter? Or was it the look of a maniac who didn't want his daughter to find out about his plot to poison the world?

Without walking into the room, Big Barney said, "How about giving me time alone with my daughter?"

Jupe, Pete, and Bob reluctantly moved out into the hallway. Jupe glanced around and then walked toward the nurses' station in the center of the hall. There was only one nurse behind the desk, the woman with the copper-red hair. Her nametag said ELIZABETH LAZAR, R.N.

"Could you tell me who was the nurse on duty last night?" Jupe asked.

"Funny you should ask," Nurse Lazar answered. "Not that it's any of your business, but it was *me*— that's who. One of the other nurses ran off and got married and I've been pulling triple shifts. Twenty-four hours straight."

Jupe smiled excitedly. "Great. Then perhaps you could tell me about Juliet Coop's three visitors," he said. "Besides her father."

Nurse Lazar frowned and shook her head. "No way. Patient info is strictly for the family."

The conversation was closed. Jupe could see it in

her eyes. She was tired, she was grumpy, she was a lot of things, but talkative wasn't one of them. Jupe sighed and looked away.

"It's really important," Bob said, running his hand through his blond hair.

She turned her stare on Bob, who smiled back.

Then he said in his most friendly voice, "Triple shifts, huh? What a bummer. How about if we personally sing you three choruses of the Beatles song of your choice—and, trust me on this, you haven't heard 'Sergeant Pepper' until you've heard us."

"Spare me the charm. I've had a long day," Nurse Lazar said. But her face actually thawed and she almost smiled. "Okay, look. There weren't three visitors last night. Only two—a young man and a young woman."

"What about the guy in the army jacket?" Jupe asked.

Elizabeth Lazar's eyebrows shot up in surprise. "I told him he couldn't go in," she said. "What a nerve! That guy gave me the creeps."

"Why?" Bob asked.

"He kept asking me questions," she said. "And he was asking some doozies."

"For example?" asked Jupe.

" 'Is she going to make it?'—he said it just like that. And 'Where is her personal property?' Questions like that. He didn't exactly look like a friend of the family, either."

"Did you get a good look at him?" Bob asked.

Nurse Lazar shook her head. "I'm not a face person," she said. "I remember his jacket and his questions. I could remember his temperature if I took it. Not his face."

"Thanks," Bob said.

As the Three Investigators turned away, Jupe said, "This Mr. Sweetness sounds suspicious to me. But maybe Juliet knows who he is. Let's go back in the room and see if she's awake."

"Hey, guys," said Nurse Lazar, shaking her head. "Juliet Coop was shaken up pretty badly, and her body needs to sleep it off. So she won't be awake for a while."

With that piece of news, the Three Investigators decided to take another approach. Jupe and Bob would do exactly what they'd done on a million other cases in the past. They'd go to Rocky Beach's police station to talk with their longtime ally, Chief Reynolds. Pete, on the other hand, would do exactly what Kelly told him to do—stay at the hospital and keep her company.

Bob jumped behind the wheel of his red VW bug, and Jupe squeezed into the passenger side.

In a little while, the two of them were sitting across from Chief Reynolds, watching him dig into his lunch—a box of Chicken Coop fried chicken.

"You guys want a piece?" the chief offered.

"Thanks," Bob said, dipping into the cardboard box, which pictured a chicken wearing a crown.

Jupe gripped his chair with both hands and tried to say "no, thanks" as calmly as he could.

"So what are The Three Investigators up to now?" asked the chief as he gnawed happily on a leg.

"We wanted to know the circumstances of Juliet Coop's accident," Jupe said.

"No mystery there," said the police chief through a mouthful of chicken. "She lost control of her car on a hill in the rain and crashed. Beginning, middle, and end."

"Isn't there anything strange about the case?" Jupe asked.

"A couple of questions to be cleared up, but there always are," said the chief. "For one thing, the accident was reported anonymously. We'd like to track down the citizen who called us. Maybe it was a witness. But why didn't he give his name? Also, there were two sets of tire skid marks—one from Juliet's car, going straight off the road, and another set beside hers. They ended farther down the hill from where she crashed."

Jupe tried to imagine it. He saw two cars coming down the hill. Juliet's car was in front and someone else—who?—was behind her. Jupe pinched his lower lip and visualized different scenarios.

"Chief Reynolds," Jupe said slowly. "Have you considered the possibility that Juliet Coop was being chased?"

3

Juliet's Romeo

"JULIET COOP BEING CHASED?" SAID CHIEF REYNOLDS, putting down his plastic cup of coleslaw and staring at the young detective. "What's your thinking, Jupe? Because that's a skinny limb you're standing on."

"It's an entirely logical possibility," Jupe said, leaning back in his chair. "If you were driving down a hill in the rain and the car in front of you skidded off the shoulder, what would you do?"

Bob spoke up first. "If I hit the brakes hard, I'd probably skid and stop down the road."

"Exactly where we found the second pair of tire tracks," Chief Reynolds added.

"But what would you do next?" Jupe asked.

"I'd probably back up the hill on the shoulder," Bob said. "That way I wouldn't have to run so far in the rain, and I could get to the other car faster."

"Exactly," Jupiter said with a triumphant smile. "Did the second car back up to try to help Juliet? Or even to find out if she was alive?"

"Not according to the evidence," the chief admitted. "We didn't find any fresh tire tracks or footprints in the soft, muddy shoulder. I'd have to say the second car just sat there."

"Who would just sit in a car and not help a driver who went off the road?" Jupe asked, and then answered himself. "Perhaps it was someone who was chasing Juliet Coop—and didn't care if she *died* in that crash!"

"It's a good theory," said Chief Reynolds. "You have any evidence?"

"We're working on it," Jupe said, standing up to leave. "Come on, Bob."

Chief Reynolds called to them before they got to the door. "Don't work too hard," he said. "As soon as the Chicken King's daughter wakes up, we'll get the whole story."

It was true, Jupe realized. When Juliet woke up, she *could* tell them whether someone had been following her before the crash. Maybe the other car had even tried to force her off the road. And maybe the driver of the other car was the person who was going to poison the chicken!

Juliet had all the answers in her sleepy head, and the Three Investigators would just have to wait.

But the real question was, would Juliet tell the truth when she woke up? If her father was somehow involved in this poison chicken thing, would she lie to protect him?

As Jupe and Bob left police headquarters and got into Bob's car, Jupe's stomach growled audibly.

"You know, Jupe, it's great that you're sticking to your diet and eveything. But no fried foods and then eating melon at every meal? It's weird," Bob said.

"Easy for you to say. Do you have a single shirt with a tag that says Extra-Large?"

Bob recognized Jupe's "discussion closed" tone of voice. "Okay. Sorry," he said. "So what's your plan now?"

"It's obvious that we have only one route to follow," Jupe answered. "Who was driving the car that was following Juliet Coop? It could have been one of the three people who visited her in the hospital last night."

"You mean Sean Fellows, Maria Gonzales, and that guy Kelly calls Mr. Sweetness," said Bob.

"Yes. And we've got to find out more about Michael Argenti, too—Big Barney's rival," Jupe said. "I can handle that with the computer back in Headquarters. I'll tap into DataServe and search their business files for everything about Michael Argenti and Roast Roost. *The Wall Street Journal* is in their data base. It should be informative. While I'm doing that, I want you to find out where Sean Fellows was last night before he came to the hospital."

"Can't handle it," Bob said apologetically. "Sax needs me at the agency."

"All right, then call Pete at the hospital and get him to take up the slack."

"No problem. But what about Maria and Mr. Sweetness?"

"I'm not too worried about Maria," said Jupe. "She doesn't seem to have any motive whatsoever. But I'll call her and check her out. As for Mr. Sweetness, we'll just have to wait until we cross paths."

Just then Jupe's stomach growled again. So Bob drove him to a supermarket to pick up another ten pounds' worth of watermelon. Then he dropped Jupe off at The Jones Salvage Yard and drove on to work. From there Bob called Pete at the hospital and gave him the assignment: Check out Juliet's ex-boyfriend, Sean Fellows.

But by the time Pete pulled himself away from Kelly, it was dark—too dark to find Sean's address. So it wasn't until Sunday that Pete pulled up in front of 23 Laurel Street, where Sean lived.

Sean Fellows' house was in a quiet and pretty neighborhood of Melton, a few miles north of Rocky Beach. The street was lined with small white wooden houses that had wide front porches and small front yards.

There was an old Bonneville convertible parked in front of Sean Fellows' house. And sitting on the porch railing was a guy with a blond flattop. He wore faded blue jeans and a white T-shirt with a leather vest. He jumped to his feet the moment Pete stepped into his yard.

"Come on!" he shouted, motioning with one hand to Pete and holding the other behind his back. "Make my day!" As soon as Pete was close to the porch, the hidden hand came out—holding a motorcycle chain!

What was going on? Pete's mind raced as his heart started thumping. Suddenly, for no reason, some maniac was coming at him with a vengeance. The guy had the motorcycle chain wrapped a couple of times around his hand, but its long tail swung freely. Pete froze in his tracks. Should he try some of his new karate moves? Or back off?

"Just you and me this time," the guy called to Pete. "That's what you want, isn't it?" His arm swung, and the tail of the vicious chain clattered and ripped into the wooden porch railing.

Forget the karate, thought Pete. He started to back away.

"I'm going to tear you open!" the guy yelled, jumping off the porch. He wasn't very big. In fact, he was much shorter and smaller built than Pete. But his voice was full of anger and he was swinging the chain wildly.

"You're making a big mistake," Pete said as he backed farther away. The guy kept coming, his black leather boots eating up the ground between them. His shoulders hulked like a gorilla's.

"I don't know what you think, but I'm looking for Sean Fellows," Pete said desperately. "I'm a friend of Juliet Coop's."

The black boots stopped walking, the chain stopped swinging.

"For real?" asked the guy.

Pete nodded his head but kept his fist clenched, ready to fight.

"Oh, well, uh, sorry," the guy said, letting out his breath. His whole body seemed to relax. "I'm Sean Fellows. I've been having some trouble here with a bunch of punk vandals. One of them just called and threatened to steal my car."

Sean motioned to the old beat-up Bonneville parked on the street. Pete stared at it.

"Maybe you should let him have it," Pete finally said with a laugh. "I mean, the tires are flat, it's leaking oil all over the ground . . ."

"Yeah, and besides that, the battery's been dead for two weeks!" Sean said, laughing too. "But I'm just sick of taking it from punks, you know what I mean?" Then he noticed his porch railing. "Don't tell me I destroyed my porch for nothing. Hey—how do you know Juliet?"

"Well, I don't really," Pete admitted. "She's in the hospital bed next to my girlfriend, Kelly."

"Oh, yeah," Sean said as he led Pete into his house. Now that he wasn't swinging a chain, Sean just seemed like a nice, average college student whose apartment had more posters than furniture.

"So why were you at the hospital so late Friday night?" Pete asked.

"Maria—Juliet's roommate in college—called me and said Juliet had been in an accident," Sean said.

"We only broke up a few months ago, Julie and I. I guess I'm not over her yet. I had to see if she was okay. Is she? Did she wake up yet?"

"Still out," Pete said. "At least, she's sleeping most of the time. The doctors say she needs a lot of rest."

Sean eyed Pete sideways for a moment. "Tell me something," Sean said, suddenly realizing that Pete was a complete stranger. "If you don't even know Juliet, what are you doing here, asking questions?"

"Kelly, my girlfriend, thinks something strange is going on," Pete said. "So I'm just checking it out. What do you know about Big Barney?"

"Big Barney? We'd still be going together if it weren't for him."

"What's that mean?" Pete asked.

"Her dad and I argued all the time," Sean said. "I'm a vegetarian, you know. No meat, no fish, no chicken. I don't believe in going around killing animals—or in anybody getting rich from slaughtering them. Barney hated my guts and he wasn't quiet about it. After a while, Juliet and I started fighting about it too. So when she said she was going to work for her father after graduation, that was about it."

"One last question and then I'll get outta here," Pete said. "How'd you get into the hospital at four A.M.?"

"I lied to the nurse, told her Julie and I were engaged," Sean admitted. "Wishful thinking, I guess."

Later that afternoon in The Jones Salvage Yard, Pete retold Sean Fellows' story to Jupe and Bob. As he talked, Pete stooped down into the engine in the back of Bob's VW. The fan belt was ancient and needed replacing. Pete was putting a new one on. Once the belt was positioned on the pulleys, he checked the tension by pressing on it with his thumb.

"It's got to give about a half inch," Pete explained. "And we'll have to tighten it up again after two hundred miles, 'cause these suckers stretch."

Ignoring the fan belt, Jupe said, "To me, the most interesting thing in Pete's account is that Sean Fellows owns a car."

"Jupe," Bob said, "sometimes I don't get you. Pete just told us a tragic story of love destroyed because of . . . of . . . dietary differences! And you shoot back with an off-the-wall comment like that."

"Remember our goal," Jupe said. "We are pursuing a suspect who was chasing Juliet Coop in a car."

"Forget Sean's car," Pete said. "The tires are flat and the battery has been dead for two weeks."

"How do you know?" Jupe demanded.

"I checked with the neighbors," Pete answered. "They confirmed his story."

"Ah." Jupe sighed. "Proof—there's no substitute for it. Still, he sounds like a fairly violent person, with that chain."

Pete shrugged as he turned the ignition on to test the engine throttle. It hummed for a minute and then made a sound something like *huppa-huppa-gak*.

"What does it mean when it makes that sound, Pete?" Bob asked.

"It's car talk for 'Trade me—I'm falling apart,'" Pete said, laughing.

Bob was used to being teased about his antique car, and he laughed too. "Could you be a little more specific?" he asked.

"All I can say is there's more wrong than I have time to fix right now. I'll have to work on it. Maybe next week. Now, what about Maria Gonzales and Michael Argenti?" Pete asked Jupe.

Jupe smiled. "I called Maria and she's got an unbreakable alibi for the time of the accident—she was trapped in an elevator with six other people. But Michael Argenti is another story. As you know, he's Big Barney's main rival. But according to *The Wall Street Journal*, Argenti recently tried to buy out Big Barney and take over the Chicken Coop restaurants."

"So the Roast Roost wants to take over the Chicken Coops!" Bob said. "Amazing! But why would Argenti try to run Juliet Coop off the road?"

"I don't know," Jupe replied. "Perhaps he was trying to get to Big Barney with a little brutal persuasion."

"Do you think he's the one who's trying to poison Big Barney's chicken?" Bob asked. "I mean, he's our only suspect."

"No—there's still Big Barney himself, and of course Mr. Sweetness, if he ever surfaces again," Jupe said.

Just then the telephone rang in Headquarters. Pete reached it first.

"Three Investigators. Pete Crenshaw," he said, flipping on the speaker phone.

It was Kelly calling from the hospital. She said only three words, but they were enough to send The Three Investigators into top speed.

"Pete," she said, "Juliet's awake."

4

Dr. Jones Operates

THE THREE INVESTIGATORS JUMPED INTO BOB'S VW and raced to the hospital, stopping only three times to make minor adjustments to major parts of the engine.

When they got there, they hurried straight to Kelly and Juliet's room. Now, finally, they were going to get the real story of what happened the night of Juliet's accident. Was someone chasing her? Was her crash an accident? What did she mean when she said someone was poisoning the chicken?

"Hey, Paul, John, and Ringo! Freeze!"

Jupe stopped, his hand on the door handle. The Three Investigators looked around and saw red-haired Elizabeth Lazar calling to them from the nurses' station.

"Sorry, you can't go in," she said, smiling at them. "Mr. Coop's in there with his daughter. And the doctors are examining Kelly. You'll have to wait. But you've got time for a couple of choruses of 'I Want to Hold Your Hand.' "

Bob laughed, but Jupe cleared his throat uncomfortably and walked away.

Five minutes clicked off on the big clock at the end of the hall. Then ten minutes. The waiting was driving Jupe crazy.

He walked over and started fidgeting with a stack of papers on the counter of the nurses' station.

"What's your hurry?" Nurse Lazar said to Jupe. She stared at his chest. "You know, you should wear something with a more positive image."

Jupe was wearing the only clean shirt he could find in his drawer that morning. It said: WHEN IN DOUBT— EAT.

"Actually we're eager to speak with Kelly's roommate, Juliet Coop," Jupe said in his most officious tone of voice. "We want to find out what she remembers about her accident."

"Well, you can forget about that," Nurse Lazar said with a little laugh. "She doesn't remember anything. She has amnesia."

Amnesia! The word hit Jupe in the gut like a ton of bricks. After all this waiting and wondering, the one person who could answer their questions had suddenly turned into a blank tape.

Finally the door to Juliet's room opened and Big Barney came out. He stood half in and half out of the doorway, wearing a purple jogging suit with a little yellow and orange chicken embroidered on the chest.

"Okay, it's settled. I'll see you tomorrow," he said to Juliet. "I'll take you home and you'll forget all about this—I mean, everything will be okay. Don't look so worried. Do *I* look worried? Of course not. *Ciao*."

Big Barney smiled and closed the door. But as soon as he started walking down the hall, the smile came off his face. He muttered something to himself as he walked quickly past the three teenagers.

"What'd he say? Could you hear?" Pete asked.

"It sounded to me like 'What am I going to do?' " Bob said.

"Let's go," Jupe said, leading the way into the hospital room.

Twenty-year-old Juliet Coop sat in her bed, propped up with pillows behind her. Her curly black hair looked tousled from sleep, but her big blue eyes were wide open and clear. Her face, however, looked uncertain.

"Hi," Kelly said cheerfully, but she gave Pete a "be careful" look. Jupe and Bob caught it as well. "Here they are, Juliet—the Three Investigators. Life-size, batteries not included, and some assembly required." Kelly giggled. "This is Jupiter Jones, Bob Andrews, and this is my Pete."

"Hi," Juliet said. Her voice was soft but raspy. "I know all about you," she said, looking at Pete.

Pete looked sideways at Kelly, while Jupe managed a shy hello.

Bob smiled and asked, "How are you feeling?"

"Like I've gone ten rounds with a boxing champ," Juliet said. "But nothing's broken, no deep cuts, just bruises and scratches. I'm actually going home tomorrow."

"That's great," Bob said.

Jupe impatiently pushed a chair from Kelly's side of the room to Juliet's bed.

"We've been very anxious to talk to you about your accident," Jupe said.

"Kelly told me. But there's something I'd better tell you first," said Juliet slowly. "I have amnesia."

"You can't remember anything at all?" Jupe asked very precisely.

"The last thing I remember is feeding my cat two mornings ago before going to work at my dad's office. Then I woke up here," Juliet said. "The amnesia's temporary. At least that's what the doctor said. It's pretty common after a big shock. My memory could come back any minute."

"If it doesn't, maybe we can help you track it down," Bob volunteered.

"So you don't remember anything from the day of the accident," Jupe mused. "What do you do in your father's office?"

"I just graduated from college with my business degree," Juliet explained. "So now I'm trying to learn Dad's business. I've been going from one department to another, doing a cost-efficiency analysis on the entire operation."

"Do you remember what departments you were studying last Friday?" Jupe asked.

"I don't," Juliet said unhappily.

"Do you remember having some bad dreams, or talking in your sleep?" Jupe asked.

Juliet shook her head.

"Guys, let's talk outside," Jupe said, motioning for Pete and Bob to follow.

Once they were out in the hallway, Jupe said bluntly, "There's no case."

"Kelly thinks there is," Pete said.

"Kelly's been sitting there for a week with nothing to do but watch television," Jupe said. "She qualifies as a certified hospital-bed potato."

"And she's obviously got a wild imagination. I mean, she's going with you, isn't she?" Bob said, giving Pete a friendly punch in the arm.

"Come on, you guys," Pete said. "Kelly knows things. She always knows what kind of clothes or lipstick and stuff to wear months before anyone else is wearing them."

"Great," Jupe said. "If we ever change our name to The Three Fashion Designers, we'll definitely make her an associate."

Pete scowled at Jupe.

"Pete," Jupe said, trying to be reasonable, "Juliet Coop had a bad accident and she had a bad dream. Now she has amnesia. I can't put those together and come up with a crime, can you?"

But it was Bob who spoke up. "I have to give you a 'maybe' on that," he said.

That caught Jupiter by surprise.

"I'll tell you why," Bob said. "I can see the crash wiping out her memory of the accident. But Juliet doesn't remember anything the day of the accident. Why is the whole day erased? Maybe something else happened."

The answer to that one was not on the tip of Jupe's tongue. He was thinking about it when Nurse Lazar's loud voice stole his attention. She was talking on the phone at the nurses' station.

"You're going to have my job?" she said with a laugh, obviously repeating what the person on the other end had threatened. "Pal, you can *have* my job and I hope you look good in the little white hat." She stamped hospital forms with a red rubber stamp as she spoke. "I'm tired of you calling every half hour asking about Juliet Coop. I've got thirty other patients to care for. You want to know how she is? Come to the hospital."

Nurse Lazar listened to the caller's reply with an angry face. "You want to talk to a doctor? Hold on." She dropped the phone loudly on the desk and walked away.

"Why would someone call so often to check on Juliet Coop?" Jupe asked.

"Because he's worried about her," Pete said.

"Right. But is he worried that she won't make it— or that she *will*? Maybe it's Mr. Sweetness," Jupe said. He cleared his throat.

"Jupe, I know that sound," Bob said. "You're deciding what voice to use."

Jupiter had a flare for acting, and he could speak in lots of different voices and styles.

"The man wants to speak to a doctor," Jupe said, smiling slyly. He picked up the receiver.

"Hello, this is Dr. Jones speaking," he said. His voice was suddenly older—exactly like a thirty-year-old's—and full of know-everything confidence.

"Never heard of you," said the voice on the other end. Smooth voice. An older man, at least middle-aged. A fast talker.

"I just joined the staff," answered Jupe. "You were asking about Juliet Coop, Mr. . . ."

Jupiter was hoping the caller would fill in the blank with his name.

Instead the man asked, "How is she?"

"Well, I'm only supposed to give out that information to the immediate family," Jupe said. "Are you a family member?"

After a pause, the man said, "I'm a friend of the family."

"A close friend?" asked Jupe.

Question and answer. Thrust and parry. Cat and mouse. The mouse ducked into another hole.

"Look, all I want to know is, is she going to be all right?" said the man.

"She has regained consciousness," Jupe said, listening carefully for the reaction on the other end of the line. "She's out of danger," he added.

"Yeah," said the voice. But it didn't sound like a happy *yeah*, or a relieved *yeah*, or even a questioning *yeah*. It sounded very much to Jupiter Jones like a that's-what-you-think *yeah*.

It gave Jupe a bad feeling. "I'll be happy to tell her you called," Jupe said, trying once more to get a name from the caller.

"That's okay, Doc," Jupe said the voice. "I'll be interfacing with her." The man hung up.

"What happened? What's wrong?" asked Pete, impatient with Jupe's silence.

"He stopped interfacing with me," Jupe said, putting the phone back on the desk just as Nurse Lazar returned with a young intern.

"The guy's a real pain," she said to the intern as she picked up the receiver. But the line was dead. "I don't believe it. He hung up!" she said in disgust.

"He's more than a pain," Jupe said softly to his friends. "He's a mystery. Something is going on and I don't understand it."

"Translation: You're not quitting after all, right?" Bob said.

"I never said I *was* quitting," Jupe replied. "I don't know what and she can't remember why, but I think Juliet Coop is in some kind of danger. And we're the only ones who know it. We've got to stay close to her."

But for the time being, they couldn't stay close to Juliet because they each had pressing things to do. Pete, who often did auto repairs for a few bucks, had to finish adjusting the ignition timing on his neighbor's Corvette.

Bob was due again at the talent agency, where he

worked part-time. One of its rock bands needed help setting up for a club date.

And Jupe had promised to check in with Mrs. Teitelbaum, the neighbor who had given him the melon diet in the first place. Mrs. Teitelbaum considered herself to be Jupe's personal one-woman diet support group.

So it was the next morning when two of the Three Investigators got together again. Jupe and Pete met at the hospital because both Kelly and Juliet were checking out.

Kelly was ecstatic to be leaving. Juliet's spirits had improved, too, but her memory still hadn't returned. She sat on her bed, waiting for Big Barney to come and take her home.

"Knowing Big Barney," Juliet said, "he'll probably show up in a gorilla suit, or bring a mariachi band to the hospital. My dad loves jokes, you know."

Ten minutes later Big Barney stuck his head in the door. "Hey! Remember me?" He was wearing a brown jogging suit and he had a fake arrow through his head.

"Dad, I've only forgotten twenty hours, not twenty years," Juliet said. "Of course I remember you. The question is: Did you remember to bring the stuff I asked for?"

Big Barney produced a small suitcase and Juliet opened it. She pulled out a pair of blue silk pajamas and held them up.

"What are these?" she asked.

"Blue silk pants and blouse," Big Barney said cheerfully. "Just like you asked for."

"Wrong closet, Dad." Juliet laughed. "These are pajamas. I can't go outside in pajamas!"

Big Barney pushed his sunglasses onto his forehead and held out the pajamas at arm's length. "Pajamas? . . . Okay, no problem," he said, the gears in his head already clicking full speed. "We just tell people you're late for a pajama party. Hahaha!" His laugh boomed through the hospital.

"No way," Juliet said, shaking her head. "If Mom were still alive, she'd punch you for even suggesting that!"

"Okay, no problem," Big Barney said. He looked Kelly over as she stood by her bed, packing to leave. "How about her? She looks about a hundred and fifteen pounds."

Kelly was amazed. "One fifteen exactly," she said. "How did you know?"

"I know how much a chicken weighs from thirty yards," said Big Barney. "Similar bone structure. I'd say your clothes would fit my Julie."

"Come on, Dad," Juliet said, embarrassed. "I can't do that. Sorry, Kelly. Sometimes he forgets that the whole world doesn't jump when he pushes an intercom button."

"Hey, it's a great idea," Kelly said. "You're welcome to borrow some clothes."

"You're a lifesaver!" Juliet said gratefully. She

closed up the suitcase Big Barney had brought. "Maybe I could borrow some makeup, too? No makeup bag, Dad," Juliet scolded. She hopped out of bed, gave her father a hug, and said teasingly, "Which one of us lost our memory, I wonder?"

"Here," Kelly said, carrying her own suitcase over to Juliet's side of the room. "Take what you want."

"Thanks," Juliet said. "I'll get them back to you."

"No rush," said Kelly.

"Hey, you know what?" Juliet said. "Dad's giving me a welcome-home party in a couple of days. Why don't you all come? It'll be a great party and you can pick up your clothes then, Kelly."

"Sounds great!" Kelly exclaimed.

Jupe also smiled, but he kept it to himself. A party at the Chicken King's house? A chance to observe Big Barney up close and personal? What could be better?

5

The Party Animal

JUPITER JONES SAT ON THE CORNER OF HIS BED AND pulled on his socks. It was the day of the party at Big Barney Coop's mansion and Jupe was nervous. This was going to be a tough assignment. Not because of the investigation—he was looking forward to that. But what was he going to say to people, more specifically, to girls at the party?

He stood up and tucked a bright polo shirt into his chinos. He faced his mirror. Not bad for a slightly overweight, medium height guy with unruly black hair. Wait a minute. Did the shirt look better tucked in or left out? It was stretching rather tightly over his stomach.

Then be began to have an imaginary conversation in his head. He was talking to a girl, the girl he'd like to meet at the party. She was petite and dainty, with short, curly hair.

"You probably haven't noticed me, but I've been staring at you uncontrollably for half an hour," said the imaginary girl with a smile.

"I notice everything," Jupe answered confidently.

"Want some chicken?" she asked, temptingly holding out a plate of Big Barney's best.

"No, thanks," Jupe said, looking into the mirror in his room. "I'm trying to lose a few."

"Gee, I really admire guys who have will power," replied the girl in Jupe's daydream.

She likes me, Jupe thought.

"Are you a friend of Big Barney's?"

"Actually I'm here to see if he's poisoning his chickens," Jupe said bluntly.

The girl's eyes opened wide. "You mean," she said excitedly, "you're a real detective?"

But by the time Jupe had tried on a more flattering shirt, his imaginary date was asking him a really tough question. "Why would someone who's made millions selling fried chicken suddenly decide to poison his own food?" she asked.

"That's a very astute question," said Jupe. "And I'm not sure of the answer. Maybe he's trying to scare off Michael Argenti. Maybe he's poisoning just a small sample of his own birds, so that when Argenti takes a sample, he'll find contamination. Or maybe he's poisoning Argenti's Roast Roost chickens as a counterattack. There are a lot of possibilities."

"You're so smart and logical," said the girl in the daydream.

"And I know judo, too," Jupe added.

"You've probably already got a girlfriend," the girl said.

"Well . . ." Jupe said.

"Hey, Jupe. Are you ready?" asked a voice from behind.

Jupe snapped out of his daydream and saw Bob standing in the doorway. He was wearing a navy-blue and red striped polo shirt and white casual pants.

"Who were you talking to?" Bob asked as they walked to his car.

"Just going over the facts of the case," Jupe answered, his face flushing.

When they arrived at Big Barney's enormous mansion in Bel Air, Pete and Kelly were waiting for them.

"Hope you brought a lot of change," Pete said. "You need bus fare to get from the front door to the pool."

The mansion was a stately forty-room, three-story stucco building with ivy growing on the walls. But that's where any semblance of elegance stopped. Everywhere there were reminders of how the Chicken King had made his millions. Instead of lawn jockeys there were chickens in jockey uniforms. The windsock on top of the flagpole was a rubber chicken. And many of the fat, round shrubs were trimmed into topiary versions of chickens wearing crowns.

The party was being held poolside, behind the mansion. There, two hundred people, young and old, were gathered around a chicken-shaped swimming pool, eating fried chicken, dancing, and having a great time.

"Remember, we're not here just to have fun," Jupe

said. "Especially you, Kelly. Be sure to 'forget' to pick up your clothes from Juliet. That way you'll have an excuse to see her again."

"I know, I know," Kelly said impatiently. "Come on, Pete, let's go find Juliet. And if I catch you having any fun, I'll tell Jupe on you." Kelly laughed as they walked away.

"Why does she take everything I say so seriously?" Jupe asked Bob.

Bob shook his head. "No—why do *you* take everything *she* says so seriously? C'mon, let's look around."

They squeezed their way through the crowd. It seemed to Jupe that everyone had a juicy drumstick or a chicken wing in their hand. They were pointing with them, waving them, even dueling with them. But most of all, they were chewing on them.

"This is torture," moaned Jupe. "When the wind blows in our direction, I can smell all eight of the herbs and spices in Big Barney's secret patented formula."

"Jupe, have some chicken," Bob said. "It won't kill you."

Bob looked at Jupe and Jupe looked at Bob, and they both winced. Maybe it wouldn't kill them, they realized—and then again, maybe it would!

"No, thanks," said Jupe.

"Hi," said a girl. She was about seventeen, with swept-back short brown hair. She had a juicy drumstick in one hand and an empty soda cup in the other.

And she was staring right at Bob. "I've been watching you ever since you came in."

Bob gave her a winning smile and said, "Don't I know you from somewhere?"

The girl laughed. "Now *there's* a new line," she said. "Sure you know me. I'm your mother."

Bob laughed and steered the girl away. "Hi, Mom. Let's go get something to drink and I'll tell you what a wonderful kid I was."

Jupe sat down in a lounge chair and watched Big Barney work the crowd like a night club comedian. Every once in a while his big voice boomed across the pool, drowning out the chatter of all the other party guests.

But suddenly another voice caught Jupe's attention. It was coming from a man standing directly behind Jupe. Jupe casually turned his head. He saw an energetic man in a white suit introducing himself to a blonde young woman who was only a few feet away.

"Don Dellasandro," the man said, handing the woman his business card.

"Peggy Bennington," said the blonde.

"It's nice to network with you, Peggy," Don said.

The more Jupe listened, the more certain he was that he recognized the man's voice.

"I'm doing some market research, Peggy," said Don. "Do you want to taste something that's going to impact on your life significantly?"

"Sure."

Don handed her a small foil-wrapped candy.

Jupe stood up to get a better view.

"Miracle Tastes?" Peggy said, reading the words on the wrapper.

"That's my company and this is my latest," said Don.

Peggy unwrapped the candy. It was a piece of chocolate. Jupe thought it looked cream-filled.

"I try to stay away from candy," Peggy said.

"But this is zero calories!" Don said with a grin. "And that's only half the miracle."

The candy was in Peggy's right hand, which Dellasandro pushed closer to her mouth. "Taste it and enter the twenty-first century." Peggy finally took a bite.

"It's really good!" she exclaimed.

Jupe's tongue was practically hanging out of his mouth. The man noticed.

"Don Dellasandro," the man said, handing Jupe his business card and a candy at the same time.

The candy was smooth and creamy and delicious.

"What do you taste?" Don asked.

"I distinctly taste three things," Jupe said. "Dark chocolate, marshmallow, and mint. No calories? How do you do it?"

"Flavorings," Don replied. "That's what Miracle Tastes is all about. I create flavors. And you did perfectamento at picking out the tastes. I'm glad I interfaced with you."

Jupe's eyes opened wide. He had been so interested

in the delicious calorie-free candy that for a second he'd forgotten about Don's voice—until that moment. But there was no doubt in Jupe's mind. Don Dellasandro was the man who had been calling the hospital every half hour to ask about Juliet Coop! "I'll be interfacing with her," he had told Jupe just before he hung up.

"I don't suppose you've got a card, do you?" Don said. "You're one heck of a taster."

"Of course he doesn't," Peggy Bennington said, laughing at Don. "He's a teenager."

As a matter of fact, Jupe thought to himself, I do have a card. But that was the last thing Jupe wanted to do—give Don Dellasandro one of his Three Investigators cards. He didn't want Dellasandro to clam up just when Jupe needed to ask him a million questions. Like, why had he called the hospital? Why was he being so mysterious on the phone? And what was Don's connection to Juliet or Big Barney?

Juliet came up to them just then and took Don Dellasandro's arm. "Don, I've got to have another candy. You didn't warn me I couldn't stop eating them," she said happily.

Don gave Juliet another piece of candy in the Miracle Tastes wrapper. "This kid is a natural taster," he said, pointing at Jupe.

"Don't steal Jupiter Jones from me," Juliet said. "Jupe and his friends are detectives, and they're going to help me figure out where I was the day of my accident."

Keep your face frozen, Jupiter told himself. Don't let on that Juliet just blew your cover.

"No kidding," Don said, looking at Jupe with narrowed eyes. "I never would have known it to look at you, pal."

Jupe had to find Bob and Pete fast. He had stumbled onto some kind of a clue, although he wasn't sure what it was.

Jupe excused himself and wandered through the crowd, looking for his friends. Near the beak end of the chicken pool there was a cluster of people, and in the middle, towering over his guests, stood Big Barney Coop. Anyone who was six feet six inches would stand out in a crowd. But that wasn't enough for Big Barney. He wore a bright-orange jogging suit with his chicken emblem stitched over his heart.

"And I said, 'I don't know. I'm still trying to figure out why the chicken crossed the road,' " Barney said with a guffaw. Laughter did not just come out of Big Barney Coop. It detonated, and when it did, even though the jokes weren't the funniest, the aftershocks made the crowd roar.

"Big Barney, just what did happen with the whipped cream chicken shortcake?" someone asked.

"What can I say. 1986," Big Barney said. "The world just wasn't ready for an all-chicken dessert. Hey, does everyone have enough to eat?"

"Actually it was 1985," Jupe interrupted. He couldn't stop himself.

Everyone looked at Jupe, including Big Barney.

"That was the year you installed water fountain hoses for washing down little kids after their meals," Jupe said.

"Hey, guy, you're absolutely on the moola," Barney said, walking over and holding out his hand to Jupe.

Jupe shook it and got a joy buzzer blast.

"Turn the page, guy," Big Barney said, putting his arm around Jupe's shoulders. "Go ahead. My life is flashing before my eyes and I'm loving every word of it."

"Well, 1986 was the year you added sugar to the French fry oil and you had live chickens marching in front of your restaurants with picket signs that said 'I'll do anything for Big Barney,' " Jupe said.

"I'm going to adopt this guy!" Big Barney announced to the crowd. "Juliet, you've got a new brother!"

While Jupe and Barney traded Chicken Coop history, Pete and Kelly were talking with Juliet. She was perched near the back of the low-diving board.

"Great party," Kelly said. "What a crowd. Who are all these people?"

"I don't know—just a bunch of people Dad invited," Juliet said. Her shoes were off and she was dipping her toes in the water. "I mean, I'm really confused, and I'm usually just the opposite—super-organized. This memory loss is driving me crazy. People keep coming up to me, saying 'Glad you're better,' and I can't tell if I don't know them or I just don't remember them."

"You haven't seen a tall, ugly guy, maybe wearing an army camouflage jacket?" asked Pete.

Juliet shook her head. "Doesn't sound like my type," she said. "Why do you ask?"

"Oh, Juliet, I forgot to tell you about him," Kelly said. "I call him Mr. Sweetness. He came to your room the night of your accident. I had the feeling you didn't know him, especially since he never showed up again."

A look of real fear crossed Juliet's brow.

"Let us worry about that," Pete said. "Hey, how's your car? I might be able to help you fix it up if it's not totalled."

"My car? Big Barney shipped it off to the junkyard real fast. He wouldn't even let me see it," Juliet said.

"And you still don't remember anything that happened to you that day?" Kelly asked.

"No," Juliet said. "Maybe something will click when I go back to work next week."

That evening after the party, the Three Investigators sat around eating pizza in Jupe's workshop at The Jones Salvage Yard. Jupe tried to stick to his diet by coming up with a compromise: After every slice of pepperoni pizza he ate two pieces of cantaloupe. It wasn't exactly a system Mrs. Teitelbaum would approve of.

"So what if Don Dellasandro called the hospital a lot?" Pete asked.

"It's the way he called, the sound of his voice, what he said," Jupe said, leaning back in his swivel chair.

"Okay, we'll find out more about him," Bob said, swigging a cola. "But what's this about having a date tomorrow?"

"We have a date with Big Barney's chickens," Jupe said. "He practically adopted me at the party. I guess he recognized a true fan. I managed to secure an invitation to visit his research lab and main offices."

"What do you think we'll find? Boxes sitting around marked 'poison'?" Pete asked, licking a piece of pizza cheese off his fingers.

"I don't know what we'll find there," Jupe answered. "It depends on how thoroughly we snoop around."

"It sounds great to me," Bob said. "But—"

"We know," Jupe and Pete said in unison. "Sax Sendler's Rock-Plus Talent Agency comes first."

"Sorry," Bob said. "Good luck, guys."

They finished the pizza, closed up the workshop, and walked outside the big iron gates of the junkyard to Bob's and Pete's cars. The sky was pink, but not for long.

"Look what's parked across the street," Pete said, pointing down the block to a black Porsche convertible. "Sixty thousand dollars on four mag wheels. An awesome machine!"

"But look at the driver—the guy leaning on the hood," Jupe said quietly. "He's wearing an army camouflage jacket. Just like Mr. Sweetness . . ."

For one second Pete froze. Then he took off running down the street toward the man. "Hey, you!" Pete shouted.

Bob and Jupe followed, but the man in the jacket hopped into his Porsche and roared away.

Instantly Pete turned back and headed for his own car. He jumped behind the wheel and zoomed down the street after the Porsche.

"Great acceleration," Pete said out loud to himself as his Scirocco pulled up right behind Mr. Sweetness's Porsche.

But as they came to the first curve and Pete hit his brakes, he suddenly wished that he weren't going so fast—because the brakes were gone. The pedal was pumping nothing but air!

Pete was speeding down a hill at 50 miles per hour, headed straight toward a busy intersection with a flashing red light!

6

Good Gravy!

F OR A MOMENT PETE COULDN'T STOP PUMPING THE brakes. They had to be working! He had checked the brake fluid himself!

But the fact was, the brakes were dead. They weren't gripping at all. And his car was picking up speed on the downgrade. It was only a matter of seconds until he'd go crashing through the intersection ahead. That is, he'd go crashing *through* it if he got lucky. More likely, he'd go crashing *into* another car crossing the intersection. After all—the flashing red light was on Pete's side, telling *him* to stop. And the other drivers had no way of knowing that Pete's Scirocco was totally out of control.

Pete's throat was so tight it felt like there was a whole apple stuck in it, instead of just his Adam's apple. His palms were sweating too.

But that didn't stop him from grabbing for the gearshift knob. He downshifted from fourth to second, hoping the drag on the engine would slow his car down. Meanwhile the black Porsche in front of him skidded into a U-turn, burned rubber, and took off.

The Scirocco slowed down, but not enough. He was only a hundred yards from the intersection. Cars were whizzing through it from the crossroad as if the yellow flasher on their side didn't exist.

Honnnnnnk! A blue Honda beeped at Pete to warn him that he was going too fast.

With his heart pounding, Pete downshifted again, grabbed the handbrake, and jerked the steering wheel to the right.

Instantly his car swerved off the road and into an empty lot where some low condominiums were being built. The rough terrain at the construction site slowed his car down—but it was a cement block, hidden in the tall grass, that brought the Scirocco to a jarring halt.

Pete's chest bounced against the steering wheel, but his seat belt kept him away from the windshield.

There goes the suspension for sure, Pete thought. He took two deep breaths to calm himself. Then he jumped out and lay down on his back with a flashlight to look under the car. Yup—the brake fluid line had been cut. Pete grabbed his keys, slammed the driver's door closed hard, and jogged back uphill in the dusk to The Jones Salvage Yard.

A couple of cans of ginger ale later, Pete's temper was finally cooling down. He and Jupe and Bob sat on chairs outside their trailer office.

"Well, we have now been introduced to Mr. Sweetness," Jupe said.

"He lived up to his name," Pete said. "The creep must have cut my brake line and then stood there just begging for me to follow him. He knew I'd hit that hill too fast if I was trying to keep up with him."

"It's a good thing you're a good driver, or we'd be The Two Investigators," Jupe said.

"Did you hear that?" Pete said, standing up and accidentally knocking over his chair. "I'm a good driver! A compliment from Jupiter Jones! You're a witness, Bob."

"Oh, I was just thinking of the expense of having new business cards printed," said Jupe.

"But seriously, guys," Bob said, "I wonder who Mr. Sweetness is and why he wants us off the case."

"It may be more pertinent to ask, how did he know we were on it?" Jupe said.

"Good point," Bob agreed. "I sure didn't see him at the party."

"And Juliet doesn't know anyone who wears an army jacket," Pete said. " 'Cause we asked her."

"Okay, so he's not a friend of the family," Jupe concluded. "Maybe he's working for someone."

"But who?" asked Pete.

It was a question they slept on that night.

The next morning, an unfamiliar car horn beeped outside Jupe's workshop and the telephone inside rang at the same time. Jupe, who had been up for hours testing electronic equipment with his oscilloscope, answered the phone while he peeked out a window. One mystery solved: The car horn was Pete's. It sounded strange because Pete wasn't driving his Scirocco. He was in his mom's car.

The telephone call was more of a surprise.

"Jupiter, it's Juliet Coop. My briefcase!" she said excitedly.

Jupe was an expert at all kinds of codes, but this one had him totally confused.

"I woke up about an hour ago and started looking everywhere for my briefcase," Juliet said after taking a deep breath. "Up until then, I'd forgotten I *had* a briefcase!"

Now Jupe was excited too. "Your memory is starting to come back," he said.

"That's one way to look at it," Juliet said. "Or you could say I'm just starting to realize how much I'd forgotten. Anyway, the briefcase isn't here at home. And I don't even know why I want to find it so badly. But I think there's something important in it. I feel like there is."

"Pete and I are just on our way to your father's office," Jupe said. "We'll keep our eyes open for it."

"Maybe I left it in my office," Juliet said. "Or in someone else's office. I'd go looking for it but Dad doesn't want me coming in for a few days. Do you think you could try to find out where I was last Friday before the accident?"

That's exactly what I was already planning to do, Jupe thought to himself.

"We'll ask around," Jupe said to Juliet. "But do you have an appointment calendar? It might give us a head start if we knew what your schedule was."

"Sure. It's a beautiful blue morocco leather diary," Juliet said wistfully. "And you're welcome to look in it yourself—if you can find it. It's always in my brief-case!"

Pete started playing his impatient symphony on the car horn again.

"I'll check out every possibility and call you tonight," Jupe said quickly.

"And I'll call you if I remember anything else," Juliet said before she hung up.

By the time Jupe got outside, Pete had the car hood raised and was peering inside the engine. He was like a compulsive dentist who couldn't resist telling every patient he came across to open wide.

"Juliet just called. She can't find her briefcase, which contains something important," Jupe announced as a greeting.

"I'll bet that's what Mr. Sweetness was hunting for," Pete said without looking up.

If Pete *had* looked up he would have seen Jupiter Jones with his jaw wide open. "Remarkable deduction!" Jupe exclaimed. "What did *you* have for breakfast?"

Then they climbed into the car and headed for Big

Barney's corporate office building in the San Fernando Valley. On the way they passed the lot where Pete's car had gone off the road. It was still sitting there.

Pete pulled into a nearby gas station and hopped out to make a phone call. He was phoning Ty Cassey, Jupe's older cousin, who usually hung around the junkyard and ran an informal car repair business whenever he was in town. Right now, however, Ty was sponging off a *different* distant relative—someone who had rented a beach house in Malibu for the summer.

"Ty?" Pete said into the pay phone. "It's Pete. Remember how you said you needed some wheels for the next three weeks? Well, I'll make you a deal. You can use my car if you'll come haul it out of the field where it's stuck."

Once Pete had arranged with Ty to take care of his Scirocco, he revved the engine of his mom's car again and they were off.

As they pulled into the parking lot at Big Barney's Chicken Coop Corporation, Pete and Jupe had to laugh. In typical Big Barney style, the building was a cross between a modern six-story office complex and an amusement park. To drive through the locked visitors' gate, Pete had to announce himself into an intercom system. But it was the same chicken-shaped intercom used at the Chicken Coop drive-thru restaurants. For a joke, Pete ordered two five-piece meals to go.

When the electronic gate swung open, Pete and Jupe drove toward the red and yellow building.

Big Barney had been at work for hours. He greeted them wearing a big smile and a red jogging suit. The first thing he said to Jupe was, "I've got one. What year did we put the carrots in the coleslaw?"

"1987," Jupe said. "Smaller containers, too."

"Didn't I tell you? Didn't I tell you?" Big Barney bellowed to anyone who was listening inside a three-county radius. "You're a nut, guy, but you're my kind of nut. However, you two will have to wear identification tags at all times. We have tight security around here." Big Barney slapped stickers on Pete's and Jupe's backs.

When they checked each other out, they discovered they were wearing KICK ME signs. Big Barney laughed so hard he almost turned as red as his jogging suit. Then he put Chicken Coop visors on both of them.

"What do you want to see first?" Big Barney asked. "My first dollar? I've got it framed and hanging over the fireplace in my office. How about my first wife? I have her hanging over the fireplace in my office too. Hahahahaha!"

"We'd like to see some of the offices, like Juliet's new office," Jupe said, trying to sound casual about it.

"I want to see where the food is made and what kind of stuff goes into it, too," Pete said.

"So you want to meet my mad scientists, do you?" Barney asked, rolling his eyes wildly. "Okay, I'll have them taken out of their cages just for you. And then I want *you*"—he pulled the visor down over Jupe's eyes—"to taste something special." Big Barney started guiding, although it was more like pushing, Jupe and Pete down the hallways. "You're not going to believe this new product. As a matter of fact, *I* don't believe it and it's my invention."

They took an elevator and toured the offices. Whenever Pete and Jupe could get away from Big Barney for a minute, they asked people if Juliet had been there on the Friday of the accident. One accountant said he had seen her that day. But he didn't remember anything about a briefcase. A few other people mentioned that they'd seen Juliet's Mustang in the parking lot when they left work—but there were no other strong leads.

Finally Big Barney took Pete and Jupe down to the basement, to a large scientific laboratory behind locked glass doors. There were warning signs saying KEEP OUT all around the electronic checkpoint entrance.

When Big Barney pushed a plastic card into an electronic box, the glass doors began to slide open. "Repeat after me," Big Barney said, looking down at Pete and Jupe. "I will tell no one about Drippin' Chicken."

"I will tell no one about Drippin' Chicken," Pete and Jupe said.

"Okay, let's get down to business. *Pandro!*" Big Barney's voice boomed and shook the glass walls of the laboratory.

Instantly a squat, burly, bald man with gold wire-rimmed glasses came marching over. He wore a long white lab jacket that had a row of Chicken Coop pins fastened above the pocket like military medals. And he actually saluted.

"Meet Pandro Mishkin," Big Barney said, pounding the man on the back. It was like pounding a mailbox. "You'll never guess where Pandro came to me from!"

I'll bet it was Disneyland, Pete thought to himself. But he played it straight and asked, "Where?"

"The Pentagon," Big Barney answered. "At least his laboratory in Washington was within five blocks of the Pentagon. Close enough."

Actually, the Pentagon is across the Potomac River in Arlington, Virginia, Jupe thought to himself. But he kept his mouth shut.

Big Barney pushed his paramilitary employee forward. Pandro Mishkin shook hands with the Investigators. His hands were clammy and cold.

"Pandro is a flavor specialist, and he's my head of R&D," Big Barney continued, using the abbreviation for Research and Development. "And if he does a really good job, I'll teach him the other twenty-four letters, too. Haha! Pandro, the boys would like an order of Drippin' Chicken."

Pandro looked at Jupe and Pete suspiciously. "Civilians, sir?" he said.

"They're okay, Pandro," Big Barney said. "What

year did we introduce wings on a string? It was right after I saw soap on a rope."

"1985," answered Pandro.

"June 22, 1985," answered Jupe.

"The guy is a walking unauthorized biography. I love him," Big Barney said. "Go get us some Drippin' Chicken, Pandro."

"Yes, sir," Pandro said. He didn't salute this time. But for a moment he did look like he wanted to click his heels together. Then he marched down the hallway toward a laboratory kitchen, using a key to unlock the door.

"What is Drippin' Chicken?" Pete asked after Pandro was gone.

"Picture this," Big Barney said. "A Chicken Coop boneless white meat chicken patty, deep fried, in a golden baked biscuit."

"I can picture it," said Jupe, almost breathlessly.

"Now, what's wrong with that picture?" asked Big Barney.

"Nothing," said Jupe. "Nothing at all."

"Where's the gravy?" asked Big Barney, grinning like a very large child with a secret he couldn't wait to tell.

"You're introducing gravy in a pump?" Jupe guessed.

Big Barney just shook his head. "The gravy," he said, savoring every word, "is *in* the chicken."

Pete was getting hungry. Jupe was absolutely awestruck.

"You get a bucket of fantabulous gravy in every bite of Drippin' Chicken," pronounced Big Barney. "My brand-new top-secret recipe puts a whole ladleful of real down-home gravy right *inside* each boneless white meat chicken patty. The American people won't know what hit them."

Big Barney's last words gave Jupe and Pete a sudden case of chills. They looked at each other. A moment ago they were salivating for Drippin' Chicken. But now both of them were thinking the same thought. Why wouldn't the American people know what hit them? Maybe it was because the Drippin' Chicken was poisoned!

It made perfect sense. Big Barney was bringing out a new product and Juliet was having nightmares. It could be a coincidence . . . but Jupe's radar told him that Big Barney's supersecret Drippin' Chicken was the subject of Juliet's fears. Her words echoed in their ears: "He's poisoning the chicken. Millions will die."

"They're nice and hot!" Pandro called from the laboratory kitchen.

"Come on, guys. I want you to be my guinea pigs," said Big Barney. "I want you to be the *first* to try Drippin' Chicken!"

7

Choose Your Poison

BIG BARNEY LOOKED AT PETE AND JUPE EXPEC-tantly. Did they realize what an honor they'd been given?

Pete looked at his watch. "It's not lunchtime," he said.

"My diet says no fried foods," Jupe said.

"No excuses!" Big Barney bellowed. "The Drippin' Chicken is hot. You guys got to learn to grab your chances—'cause you never know when your timer is going to start beeping, telling you you're cooked!"

There was no way they could get out of tasting the Drippin' Chicken without seeming very suspicious. So Jupe and Pete started slowly walking down the hallway. Holding a tray, Pandro left the lab kitchen and steered them into his office across the hall. Fortunately Big Barney didn't follow them into the room. Instead, he called Pandro back out into the hallway for a quick huddle.

Inside Pandro's office, on his modern glass and

steel desk, sat two steaming Drippin' Chicken biscuit-sandwiches.

"They look superb," Jupe said.

"Are you nuts? They could be poison. We've got to lose them. Put 'em in your pockets," Pete said.

Jupe looked down at his blue jeans, which were already a little on the tight side. "Are you kidding?"

"Well, we can't use the wastebasket," Pete mumbled. "They'd find them. And I'm wearing jogging pants without pockets."

"The couch?" Jupe said.

Pete shook his head. "They'd smell them and *then* they'd find them. Your pockets—quick!"

Pete pointed and Jupe obeyed. The gravy oozed out and started running down his leg. "I'll watch the door for Pandro," Pete said. "See what you can find."

Jupe looked around the office for Juliet's briefcase. It wasn't behind or under the desk or in any of the drawers. And the file cabinets were locked. So Jupe switched gears and began looking for anything else of interest.

"Hey, look at this," Jupe said. "Pandro's desk calendar has a page torn off. Six days ago."

"That's Friday, the day Juliet can't remember," Pete said. "And the night of her accident."

"We've got to find out if there's a connection," Jupe said. Just then he heard footsteps approaching. "Be sure to argue with me about the calendar," Jupe whispered to Pete.

Pete nodded. A split second later Pandro strode back into the room. "At ease, men. Good gravy, you two demolished those fast," Pandro said. "You must have really loved our Drippin' Chicken."

"I can honestly say I've never eaten anything like it," Jupe said.

"The General is going to be happy to hear that," Pandro said, referring to Big Barney. "He sends his apologies. Had to go take care of business."

"Did you invent Drippin' Chicken?" Jupe asked.

"No." Pandro shook his head. He sat down behind his desk. "The General went out of house for this one. I told him not to, at first. I said we could handle it right here. But he pulled rank on me and went right to the top. He got Don Dellasandro of Miracle Tastes to develop Drippin' Chicken. I like to say it was the Chicken King and the Flavor King working on the same team."

"So you don't know what's in it?" Pete asked.

"Of course I do," Pandro said. "It was my job to analyze the secret gravy recipe and make certain it contained just exactly what Mr. Dellasandro said it did. Then I gave my personal go-ahead to the General. That's how I got my tenth bird." One of Pandro's stubby fingers pointed to the last silver chicken pin on his lab coat. "But of course it's all classified material. I can't tell you anything else."

"We wouldn't want you to," Jupe said. "Just coming here is exciting enough. After all—we didn't even know Big Barney until *eight* days ago, did we, Pete?"

Pete looked at Jupe blankly. Then he saw that Jupe's eyes were on the desk calendar. "You mean *six* days ago, don't you, Jupe?" he asked with a smile.

"Eight days," Jupe said, shaking his head.

"You're wrong," Pete said, walking over to Pandro Mishkin's desk and flipping the pages of the desk calendar. "It was six days ago. Last Friday. I'm sure of it—hey, the page is missing."

"I know," Pandro said. His voice was automatic, as though he already knew what he was going to say. "I always write my grocery lists on the calendar and take them with me."

"Well, we won't take up your time any longer," Jupe said. "We've got to get home and change our clothes."

Pete started choking and coughing to cover up a laugh. But Jupe was right. The gravy stain on his pants pocket was starting to spread and show.

They found their way out of the office complex and headed home. The Drippin' Chicken went into the nearest trash can.

That evening cartons of Chinese food were stacked like the Great Wall of China in Jupe's workshop. Pete, Jupe, and Bob were having a six-course conference about the case, filling Bob in on everything they'd seen and everyone they'd talked to at the Chicken Coop Corp. that afternoon.

"Well, it sounds like maybe we know the 'what'— the probable poisoning target is Drippin' Chicken," Bob said. "At least that's our best guess up to now. But that still leaves four questions: who, where, when, and how? And there's still the possibility that Michael Argenti is up to something weird."

"We didn't find Juliet's briefcase, so we still don't know what that has to do with anything," Jupe said, rolling up and eating fat pancakes stuffed with moo shu pork and honeydew melon.

"No one even remembered seeing Juliet last Friday—except one old guy," Pete said. "And he wasn't too swift. I bet he was remembering a totally different day."

"Where'd we get this food?" Bob asked suddenly.

"Usual place," Pete said. "Sun Yee Chinese Deli. Why? What's wrong?"

"I'm not crazy about their fortune cookies," Bob said, staring hard at the small paper fortune in his hand. He passed it over to Pete and Jupe.

On the paper was a handwritten message that said:

The food you've just eaten could have
been poisoned. Next time it will be!
Stay away from the Chicken King!

8

A Word from Our Sponsor

JUPE FINISHED READING THE THREATENING FORTUNE cookie message and passed it back to Bob. No one said anything for a moment. They just sat there feeling watched . . . and very vulnerable.

Then Jupe grabbed the other two fortune cookies. The same message was inside all three.

Bob pushed his carton of shrimp fried rice to the far side of the table. "Nothing like a death threat to ruin your appetite," he said.

Pete reached for the telephone.

"Who are you calling?" Jupe asked.

"Sun Yee's restaurant. To find out who did this."

"Good idea," Bob said.

"No, it isn't," Jupe countered. "Don't bother, Pete."

"Why not?"

"Because I'm certain I know what happened," Jupe answered slowly. But he didn't go on.

"Well?" Pete said finally. "What's your theory, Jupe?"

"Well," Jupe said reluctantly, "I think a waiter at the restaurant probably stuffed that message in the cookie. And he probably did it because someone came into the restaurant and paid him five dollars to help out with a little practical joke."

"How do you know?" Pete asked.

"I know, that's all. Trust me," Jupe said.

"Of course we trust you," Bob said. "It's just that—"

"—we know you too well," Pete said, finishing Bob's sentence. "So, like, we know when you're hiding something."

"Okay, okay," Jupe said. "I know the setup with the fortune cookies because I've done it sometimes myself—for a joke, of course."

"So *that's* why your fortunes always say things like 'You are brilliant, handsome, and a leader,' while ours always say 'Try harder to be like your intelligent friend'! " Bob said.

"Oh, brother!" Pete exclaimed, throwing his crumpled-up napkin at Jupe's chest.

"It was just a joke!" Jupe insisted. "There's no similarity between my occasional humorous pranks and this . . . this . . . death threat." Jupe was quiet for a moment while those last words sank in. "The salient point," he went on, "is that this message is the *second* warning we have received. It tells us that Pete's cut brake line was not just an isolated incident—that it was probably related to our investigation into the

Chicken King. Something sinister *is* going on. And we'd better be on our guard from now on, because someone is watching us."

"I'll bet the guy who did this wears army fatigues and drives a black Porsche convertible, right?" Pete asked.

"I wouldn't be surprised," Jupe said. "He certainly knows a lot about us."

The phone rang just as Jupe finished his sentence. It startled all three of them.

"The Three Investigators. Jupiter Jones, founder, speaking."

"Just the badger I want to talk to!" boomed the voice on the other end. "You have the honor of talking to Big Barney Coop!"

"It's Big Barney," Jupe said with his hand over the receiver.

"What's he calling about? Does he know about the Chinese food?" Pete asked.

Jupe shook his head and motioned for Pete to be quiet.

"Listen, guy," Big Barney said into the phone. "I've got big news with a capital Big. Tomorrow yours ever so truly is taping the first Drippin' Chicken TV commercials. I'm talking landmark Chicken History. I want you there, guy. Can't do it without you."

Jupe couldn't believe his good luck. Big Barney was issuing an invitation to do exactly what Jupe wanted to do—hang around and see what Big Barney was up to.

"Where? And when?" Jupe asked.

"Maltin Mix Studios on Alta Vista Drive. One o'clock. I like my team on time."

Then he was gone.

Late that night, after Pete and Bob had left, Jupe watched a videocassette he had made of Big Barney's TV commercials. Barney always sat at a cluttered desk in what looked like a combination office, library, and game room. Sometimes he interviewed guests or read fan letters. But Jupe's favorites were the more unpredictable commercials. Like the time during Big Barney's "Hate a Hamburger Week," when Big Barney threw a whipped cream pie in a cow's face. Or the time Big Barney sat with his back to the camera during the entire commercial because he was angry at the audience for forgetting his birthday.

But Jupe's absolute favorite was the commercial Big Barney made to promote his two new styles of chicken—Cracklin' Crunchy and Burning Barbecue. Big Barney paid a Las Vegas minister to perform a quickie wedding ceremony for two chickens! The picture of one chicken dressed in a tuxedo and the other in a lace wedding dress, with Big Barney standing there as the best man, said just about everything there was to say about Big Barney.

After watching the tape Jupe went to bed, but he spent a restless night. He couldn't stop wondering whether Big Barney was the person whom Juliet had been talking about in her sleep. And was the Drippin' Chicken the product he planned to poison? Or was it something else? Was Big Barney really going to make a commercial to promote a product that could kill millions?

At one o'clock sharp the next afternoon, Bob and Jupe arrived at Maltin Mix Studios just outside of Beverly Hills. Two minutes later, Pete and Kelly pulled up in Kelly's mother's car.

"Look at that," Bob said to Jupe. "You've been complaining all the way over here about not having your own car. But when Pete, of all people, doesn't have a car, what can you expect?"

"Okay," Jupe replied. "I'll stop complaining until Pete gets his car fixed. Then I'll start again."

When they got inside, Juliet met them at the entrance to studio A, wearing a Chicken Coop visor over her curly black hair.

"Hi. Dad's been asking about you," she said to Jupe with a smile. "Have you found out anything new?"

"No," Jupe said. "But according to a fortune cookie we got last night, we're on the right track."

"Good," Juliet said. "I hope you find my briefcase soon. I still can't remember what's in it. But I *want* it! It's becoming an obsession."

Then she took Jupe, Bob, Pete, and Kelly into the glass production booth at one end of the studio, where they could watch the taping. Lots of people from Big Barney's office were there, including Pandro Mishkin, the flavor specialist.

The desk on the set for Big Barney's commercials was piled high today with letters, empty Styrofoam coffee cups, rubber chickens, crayon drawings of fried chicken sent in by a class of third graders, and a photo of Juliet as a child in a Halloween chicken costume.

Finally the director called over the PA microphone, "We're ready. Could someone go get Big Barney out of makeup?"

A minute later Big Barney made his entrance, wearing a jogging suit with alternating red, white, and blue stripes. On his face he wore a rubber chicken beak which covered his nose and upper lip. He carried with him a large antique silver tray with a heavy, ornate silver lid. He squinted against the bright lights, trying to see into the booth.

"Is my guy here?" he called.

"He's here, Mr. Coop," the director said, looking back from his swivel chair at Jupe. The Investigator was wearing his official Big Barney 10 Year Anniversary T-shirt. It had a drawing of a chicken's body with Barney's head.

"Pandro said you went creamed corn over the Drippin' Chicken sample," Big Barney called out. "I've got plenty for everybody today."

"Too bad you wore your good pants," Pete whispered to Jupe.

Once Big Barney was seated comfortably with his feet on the desk, the studio settled down and the director announced, "Quiet please. Drippin' Chicken. Take one!"

And Big Barney began to talk, looking into the

camera as if he could see through it to the people watching TV.

"Hey, guy," he said. "This is your friend and mine, Big Barney Coop. You know that I don't make commercials unless I've come up with some new way for you to make me rich. Well, this time I've got to tell you that I've outdone even myself. Okay, I wasn't there when they invented the wheel. And I wasn't there when they invented penicillin. And I wasn't there when they invented the paper clip. History didn't call me at those momentous moments. Or if it did, I didn't get the message, which is why I'm firing my secretary. Hahahaha! But today you and I are not only going to make history, we're going to eat it."

At that point, Big Barney uncovered the silver tray to reveal a mountain of steaming-hot Drippin' Chicken biscuit-sandwiches. Even the crowd in the production booth began to ooh and aah hungrily.

Big Barney picked up one of the sandwiches and brought it close to his mouth. The camera moved in for a tight shot. The Three Investigators gulped. Was he really going to eat one?

"I have done what people have been trying to do since the dawn of civilization—or maybe the sunset of civilization. I have created Drippin' Chicken, the chicken with a bucket of unbelievable, irresistible gravy in every bite. And get this—the gravy is *inside* the sandwich! That's right. Now there's nothing to get in the way of your having major gravy stains down the front of your shirt. I told my guys, this time let's give people something they never expected in their sandwich. Well, we've done it, and I can't wait for you to gobble it down. Like this!"

Then he did it. Big Barney took a big bite out of the Drippin' Chicken sandwich he was holding. And with gravy dripping down his chin, he gave the camera a big smile.

"Cut," yelled the director. "Great!"

Some of the bright lights in the studio dimmed and people in the booth relaxed.

Kelly leaned over and said to the Investigators, "That was hysterical!"

But Jupe, Pete, and Bob were still watching Big Barney through the studio glass. And they saw him spit out the bite of Drippin' Chicken without even chewing it!

It was as if Big Barney were confessing that Drippin' Chicken was poisonous—too poisonous to be eaten by any human being!

9

Fowl Play

JUPE KNEW ENOUGH ABOUT THE TELEVISION BUSI-ness to know that the taping session for Drippin' Chicken wasn't over yet. But he didn't expect it to go on for another five hours. Big Barney did the commercial twenty times more. And at the end of each take Big Barney took a big, squishy bite of Drippin' Chicken, which he promptly spit out when the director yelled "Cut."

When it was all over, Big Barney yelled, "Let's party!" and invited everyone in the studio to dig in and enjoy the Drippin' Chicken samples. There was a microwave off to one side so the samples could be heated up. The camera crew, floor crew, and production people in the booth all rushed up to pig out on the hot biscuits filled with chicken and gravy.

Jupe watched carefully.

No one was dropping dead. No one was writhing with stomach cramps or chills or any of the other symptoms of poisoning. The only moans Jupe heard were the sounds of ecstatically happy people raving about the delicious taste.

Slowly Jupe walked over to the desk where the Drippin' Chicken sat invitingly on the silver tray. There were only two sandwiches left. Just as he reached for one of them Bob poked him on the shoulder. "Notice who's not eating the samples?" he asked.

Jupe looked around.

"Big Barney and Mishkin," Bob said. "Why is it the two people who know the most about Drippin' Chicken are the two people who aren't eating it?"

Jupe hesitated—and lost his chance.

"Excuse me," said a young woman. She reached in front of Jupe and grabbed both sandwiches. "I was going to take one to my boyfriend, but they're too irresistible." She gobbled up both of them right in front of Jupe's face.

Jupe gave Bob a look of pure frustration, but he maintained a calm and rational voice. "Oh, well. If it turns out that they're not harmful, I'll have plenty of opportunities to try them fresh from the Chicken Coop."

When the party started to wind down, the Three Investigators ducked out for some fresh air. They leaned against their cars, waiting for Kelly and Juliet and deciding what to do next.

Finally Kelly and Juliet came out of the studio and into the parking lot. Kelly was brushing her long brown hair as they walked. "I'm going with Juliet to pick up the clothes I left at her house," Kelly said.

Jupe didn't like that. He still wanted Kelly to have a reason to keep in touch with Juliet. When he thought Juliet wasn't looking, he shook his head at Kelly. She must have gotten the message because she gave him a small wink and a nod before she got into Juliet's car.

"There goes the Chickenmobile," Pete said. He pointed to a specially built yellow and orange Cadillac convertible with a giant three-dimensional Chicken Coop emblem on the hood. Big Barney beeped the horn as he drove off. It played a cock-a-doodle-do.

"Where's *he* going?" Jupe asked.

"Maybe he's just going to dinner," Pete said.

"Sneaking off to McDonald's?" Bob joked.

"You follow him, Pete," Jupe said, giving orders as usual. "Bob and I will tail Pandro Mishkin. If we're lucky, one of them will lead us to something useful."

Pete drove away in Kelly's car. Bob and Jupe climbed into Bob's VW to wait for Pandro Mishkin to leave. After a while Pandro got into a long Lincoln Town Car, which had a Chicken Coop logo painted on the side, and drove away.

Bob and Jupe followed him for several hours, first to a seaside restaurant where Mishkin had dinner alone, and finally to a small house set back on a very steep hill in an area called Sugarloaf Canyon. It was getting dark by the time they arrived. Sugarloaf Canyon looked like a community planned for people who hated to have neighbors. The houses were hard to get to and set very far apart.

Jupe and Bob parked down the hill from Mishkin's house, wondering what their next move would be.

"Look—he didn't go inside," Bob said as they watched through the thick bushes that surrounded Mishkin's large house. "He's walking around to the back."

"Let's go," Jupe said, climbing out of the Volkswagen with relief after so much time in the cramped car.

They waited a minute to let Pandro get ahead. Then they walked up his long driveway and past the low stucco house, following the path he had taken. All the lights in the house were dark, but at the back they saw an outdoor light shining down from a tree.

"There's a fence," Jupe said. "And from its style and height, I would surmise that there's a swimming pool behind it."

No sooner had Jupe made that pronouncement than he and Bob heard splashing sounds.

"Come on, baby, you can do it," said the familiar voice of Pandro Mishkin. "Come on, my little Petunia. Hup, two, three! Swim!"

More splashing sounds wafted through the soft summer air. The light on the tree cast an eerie glow as it shone through the slots in the wooden fence.

"Who's he in there with?" Bob wondered out loud. He and Jupe looked at each other, puzzled.

"Shall we find out?" Jupe asked softly.

Bob nodded and the two of them approached the gate to the pool area. They opened it noiselessly and slipped inside. A small outdoor shower and equipment house blocked their view of the deep end of the pool. Jupe led the way as they crept around the structure to get a better look.

But suddenly Jupe's foot got caught on a plastic hose. He fell with a loud crash onto a poolside deck chair. One instant later, Jupe and Bob found out who Pandro Mishkin's swimming companions were. Terrible barking, growling, splashing sounds erupted— and two huge Dobermans leaped out of the pool!

"Charge! Enemies in the camp!" Mishkin yelled from the pool. "Sic 'em, Petunia! Get 'em, Zeus! Don't take any prisoners!"

Jupe scraped his hands scrambling up to escape the frantic Dobermans. He stumbled desperately toward the gate. Bob was way ahead of him. They ran as fast as they could, screaming for help the whole time. But who was going to hear them? The neighbors were miles away.

The barking got louder and louder. Where was the gate? Had someone moved it? In reality, it was only a few feet away, but Bob and Jupe felt like they'd been running forever.

Finally Bob and Jupe reached the gate. They ran through it and Bob slammed it shut, locking the dogs inside. But he and Jupe kept running, down the driveway to Bob's car.

"Close one," Bob said, jumping behind the wheel.

Bob peeled away from Mishkin's house so fast that even his little VW kicked up some stones. Jupe's heart was still racing when they were several miles down the road.

Finally Jupe caught his breath long enough to start acting like himself again—which meant analyzing the situation and giving orders. "We didn't learn much," he said. "But we did find out that Mishkin has fairly tight security at home. I wonder why? Let's get back to Headquarters. We have some plans to make."

Later that night in Jupe's workshop, he and Bob told Pete and Kelly about Pandro Mishkin and his swimming Dobermans.

Then it was Pete's turn to report. "I followed Big Barney to a takeout salad restaurant called Veg Out. He bought a chef's salad, took it with him, and drove to Don Dellasandro's office building."

"Miracle Tastes?" Jupe said.

"You got it," Pete said. "Dellasandro's got a building with offices, labs, and a warehouse down in Long Beach."

"How's the security?" Jupe asked.

"The guards look harmless," Pete said. "But the security system on the entrance is a monster. Lots of alarms and a computer keypad to get in."

"Well, I was a real klutz about handling my assignment," Kelly said with a laugh. "Just as Juliet was giving me back my clothes, somehow, just by 'accident,' I managed to spill my iced tea all over them. Juliet felt so bad, she offered to have them dry cleaned herself. I can pick them up at her house tomorrow."

"Or perhaps the next day, or the next," Jupe said,

smiling. "Good work, Kelly." Jupe's head suddenly turned toward the front door of the workshop. He put his finger to his lips and motioned for Pete to follow him. They moved quietly and took positions on each side of the door. Then Jupe opened the door with a jerk.

Outside in the dark there was no one, but there was a box. It was about the size of an extra-large shoe box. It was wrapped in plain brown paper and tied with a red string, and it was lying right in front of the door. The handwriting on the paper said "For Jupiter Jones." Pete scooted the box with the toe of his sneaker, pushing it farther away.

"Feels heavy," he said.

Jupe bent down and picked up the package. "It *is* heavy," he said.

"You going to open it?" Bob asked as Jupe carried it into the workshop, leaving the door open.

"Don't," Kelly said, holding Pete's arm.

Jupe listened carefully for a minute, first to the box and then to the sounds in the night air. Was someone still out there? Pete and Bob listened, too, and their leg muscles tensed, ready to spring into action.

Finally Jupe untied the string. The box seemed to move in his hands. "Whatever's in here is moving around, because the balance of the box keeps changing." Jupe unwrapped the brown paper. But he was holding the box with the lid facing down, so the contents spilled out onto Jupe's feet.

Splat!

Kelly screamed and Jupe's face went white.

There, lying on Jupe's new white sneakers, was a dead chicken—with its head cut off! It was floppy and freshly-killed, with a big smear of blood at the neck. Then Jupe saw the note, also stained with chicken blood. Slowly he picked it up. It said:

> *Jupiter Jones—*
> *You're already plump enough to be*
> *slaughtered. Stay away from things*
> *that aren't your business! This is*
> *your last warning!*

10

Just Us Chickens

BOUNCE . . . BOUNCE . . . BOUNCE . . . IN THE warm morning sunshine, Pete dribbled around Jupe and made a break for the basketball hoop above his garage door. He went up for a back-handed lay-up and all 190 pounds of him stuffed the ball through the net.

"Come on, Jupe," Pete said, passing the basketball back to him. "Are you playing?"

"I keep thinking about last night and that chicken," Jupe said.

"You're telling me," Pete said, coming up to Jupe. "Yuck—it's enough to give us nightmares for a week. That's why you've got to get some exercise. It'll take your mind off having to wash all that blood off your shoes."

Jupe gagged, remembering the horrible sight of the headless chicken, dripping blood and veins. While he was trying to catch his breath, Pete knocked the ball out of his hands and went in for another lay-up.

"Let's not relive the moment," Jupe said with a

shudder. "The question is, who sent it? Who wants us to stay away from Big Barney? It doesn't seem like the kind of thing Big Barney would do himself. He's giving us other signals—inviting us to come closer, to get involved with his business."

"Jupe," Pete said seriously, "you'll figure it out. You always do. I have faith."

Jupe smiled at his friend and quickly stole the ball from him. Jupe threw a long, arching shot toward the basket—and missed by a mile.

"You're getting closer," Pete said. "You're definitely in the same state."

Bob's car horn beeped in the driveway and he hopped out as soon as the VW chugged to a stop.

"Morning, guys," Bob said. "Seen the paper, Jupe?" He tossed Jupe the morning edition. "Check out the front page of the business section."

Pete tossed Bob the basketball and they shot a few while Jupe read the news story.

"This is extremely timely," Jupe said a few minutes later. "Michael Argenti has intensified his efforts to acquire the Chicken Coop restaurants. Hmmm . . . I've got to make a phone call." He disappeared into Pete's house.

Five minutes later he came out, wearing the famous Jupiter Jones I-told-you-so smile.

"Who'd you call?" asked Pete.

"Michael Argenti," Jupe said. "I thought it was time that we checked him out. After all, it's possible that he won't succeed in buying the Chicken Coop restaurants. In which case, he might settle for merely ruining Big Barney's business by poisoning his food."

"What'd Argenti say about that?" asked Pete.

"I didn't talk to him," said Jupe. "His secretary said he was out of town today. And do you know where?"

"No, but you'd better know or this is a really dumb conversation," Pete said.

"Petaluma," Jupe announced. "Just north of San Francisco. It's where Big Barney has his chicken farms."

In less than an hour Jupe and Pete were climbing aboard a commuter plane to San Francisco. They had phoned Juliet and gotten her to agree to pay all their expenses in this investigation—although she didn't realize that they were also investigating her father. Bob stayed behind because he had some heavy-duty responsibilities at the talent agency. One band was scheduled to play at two different weddings that day, and Bob was supposed to make sure that the band didn't get too drunk to make it to the second wedding reception on time.

At San Francisco International Airport, Pete and Jupe rented a car and drove an hour north to Petaluma. They had no trouble finding Big Barney's ranch. It was well marked and well known to everyone in town.

The ranch itself looked more like an automobile factory than a chicken farm. There were two huge cinderblock buildings, each two stories high and about as long as a football field. Surrounding them was a chain-link fence.

Pete and Jupe stood outside the fence for a moment and stared. Maybe because it was Saturday, no one was around. So the guys opened the gate and walked fifty yards to the first building. A quick check to see if anyone was watching—then they sneaked inside.

They couldn't believe their eyes—or their ears. Inside they saw not hundreds of chickens, but hundreds of *thousands* of them in a well-lighted space. The noise was incredible. Light poured in through a greenhouse-style glass roof, but air conditioning kept the temperature down.

Jupe and Pete grabbed two Chicken Coop visors that were hanging on a peg by the doorway. They put them on so they'd look like employees and started to snoop around.

The first thing they found out was that it was very difficult for human beings to move in this building. Besides the countless chickens, there were long red plastic pipes mounted a few inches from the floor—and they were everywhere. The pipes ran the entire length of the building, like long, low hurdles. Pete and Jupe had to step over them to walk around. These were feeding pipes, with small red plastic bowls attached every eighteen inches. There were also water pipes, with small purple nozzles for the birds to drink from. The entire process of chicken raising was automated, which was why no people were around.

The birds were grouped into long sections according

to age, from little purple fuzzy chicks up to fat, full-grown, bright-plumed birds. Pete and Jupe walked from section to section.

"Why do some of them look so strange?" Pete asked. "Look at that guy—he's got the weirdest little wings I've ever seen."

"Genetic engineering," Jupe said. "A process of planned nutrition and selective breeding so that desirable physical and biological traits become dominant. Some are bred so their wings are big and some so they have big breasts to produce a lot of white meat. That's why that one looks top-heavy, like it's going to fall over."

Suddenly Jupe and Pete saw they were not the only humans in the building. Three men had entered and were looking around. They were standing where Jupe and Pete had come in, among the smallest chicks.

"Quick," Jupe said. "Look busy."

"There's nothing to do," Pete said. "Everything's done by machine."

"Then hide!"

Jupe and Pete ducked down behind a partition that separated one breed of chickens from another. It was a low partition, and they could see over the top of it to watch and eavesdrop on the men who had come in. But the chickens were crowding around them, pecking at their legs.

"I've got to get out of here," Jupe said, suddenly feeling claustrophobic. "Every time I see the white ones, I remember that package we got last night."

But just then the three men moved closer to the guys. One of them wore a red plaid shirt and khaki pants. His white cap, with the Chicken Coop emblem on it, said HANK in big red letters. The other two men looked totally out of place. They wore dark blue suits, and one had mirrored aviator sunglasses. He was young, with short dark hair. When he removed his sunglasses, his blue eyes were like the flames of a blowtorch.

Then Jupe heard Hank say, "Anything else I can show you, Mr. Argenti?"

Michael Argenti? This was one conversation Jupe had to hear!

Michael Argenti looked right through Hank and talked only to the other blue-suited man. "I've seen enough," he said in a dissatisfied tone of voice. "Make some notes and write up a memo. I'm going to have to make some real changes around here. I can see that."

"Yes, Mr. Argenti," said the eager assistant, digging out a pen and small notebook from his jacket pocket.

Michael Argenti put his mirrored sunglasses back on and looked at Hank. "What's your output?"

"From hatched egg to slaughter in nine weeks," Hank said. "We get fifty thousand full grown about every week."

"Not enough. The population's got to be doubled," Michael Argenti said.

The assistant wrote that down.

"Big Barney doesn't like the birds too crowded," said Hank.

"This isn't a rest home for chickens," said Michael Argenti with a nasty smile. "It's a factory. The more units we turn out, the more money we make. At Roast Roost we get mature birds in seven weeks. You're going to have to be that good, too."

Michael Argenti looked around the plant again, shaking his head. Then he bent down and took a handful of grain out of one of the feeding bowls. Little chicks pecked at it in his open palm. Michael Argenti looked back at Hank. "The feed's gotta change, too. But I'll take care of that personally," he said. "I've got something special in mind."

By that time, the assistant had the door to the outside standing open. Michael Argenti walked through it and climbed into a stretch Mercedes limo without breaking his stride. As the car drove off Jupe read its license plate.

It said PLUCKER-1.

11

Bumper Cars

"**W**ELL, MICHAEL ARGENTI WAS EVERYTHING I EX-pected him to be," Jupe said to Pete as they drove south, heading back toward San Francisco. "A brash, arrogant, ruthless, self-important business animal."

"Just what I was thinking," Pete said. "But you left out the word 'jerk.' "

They rode in silence for a while, but around 7:00 P.M., when they were just a few miles outside of the city, Jupe suddenly yelled at Pete, "Pull over!"

"What's wrong?" Pete asked as he steered their small rented car onto the highway off-ramp. Then Pete saw the sign. It was a tall painted chicken with a flashing neon crown, perched on the purple barn roof of a Chicken Coop restaurant. "What happened to a melon a day keeps the pounds away?" Pete asked.

"There have been a number of scientific studies lately which have hypothesized that foods rich in saturated fats may actually be beneficial to people," Jupe said.

"That's barn crud and you know it," Pete said. "But so is your melon diet. So let's eat!"

Pete parked the car and caught up with Jupe, who was not wasting a second getting into the Chicken Coop restaurant.

Jupe stopped at the doorway, inhaling deeply. "Did you know that the sense of smell is one of the weakest of the five senses?" he told Pete. "After you've been in a particular aroma for even a short period of time, you become dulled to it and can't smell it anymore. That's why it's important to savor that first blast of grease when you walk in the door."

"Give me a break, Jupe. People are waiting behind us to get in," Pete said.

They walked to the order counter, where a teenage girl in a purple plaid shirt and a khaki skirt stood smiling at them. She wore a white cap that didn't have a bill. It had a beak. According to the purple writing on her hat, her name was Carly. Carly gave them the official Big Barney greeting.

"Hi there, buddy. Hi there, friend. It's great to have you back again," she said. "What's your order? What's the scoop? We've got it from hen's teeth to soup. What would you like?"

"I'll have a six-piece murder to go," Pete said absently.

"Excuse me?" the girl said.

"Oh—sorry," Pete said. "Six-piece chicken."

Then Jupe ordered a full chicken dinner and the two of them found a table by the window. But when they sat down to eat, Pete didn't touch his food.

"You know," Pete said, "we're making a pretty big assumption here. I mean, what if *this* food—that drumstick you're about to demolish—is the stuff that's poisoned?"

"I haven't forgotten and I haven't ruled out the possibility," Jupe said. "But there are times in a man's life when he just has to take a risk—and this is one of them." He bit into the drumstick and closed his eyes to savor it.

Pete shrugged his shoulders and picked at his own food.

"The key to this case is Juliet Coop and, quite possibly, her missing briefcase," Jupe said when he had eaten a few more bites. "Unfortunately, we can't wait for her amnesia to pass to find a solution. Our poisoner knows we're on the case, and if he can't scare us away, he may decide to speed up his plans. So let's consider what MOM has to say about our three suspects."

"My mom would say, 'Don't get into any more trouble, Pete. You've given me enough gray hairs already,' " Pete said.

"Not that kind of mom," Jupe said. "I was referring to that classic formula for all detection: Motive, Opportunity, and Means. Now, as for Big Barney, he certainly has the means and the opportunity to poison his food. He could introduce something into the birds' diet or inject the birds during processing."

Pete looked down at the chicken in his hand and dropped it onto his tray.

"But what is Big Barney's motive?" Jupe went on.

"He's nuts," Pete said.

"Is he nuts enough to kill millions of people and injure his own daughter?" Jupe asked.

"I don't know," Pete replied. "But who else would send you a chicken with its head cut off?"

"Anybody can buy a chicken. And we can't forget that Michael Argenti is in the chicken business too," Jupe said. "*There* is a man with an irrefutable motive. I'd say he's determined to either take over Big Barney's business—or ruin it. If the takeover deal goes through, fine. But if it doesn't succeed, maybe he's planning to poison Big Barney's chickens as some sort of revenge. Maybe his visit to Petaluma today was really a matter of casing the joint to figure out how to poison the feed. That would cover means. And as for opportunity, it seems like anyone has access to Big Barney's ranches. After all, *we* walked right in, no questions asked."

"Okay, how about suspect number three?" said Pete.

"Mr. Sweetness? Your guess is as good as mine. He's fronting for someone—but who?"

They pondered the suspects as they dumped their trash in a chicken's mouth garbage can and then headed for the car.

It was dark outside as Jupe and Pete drove into San Francisco. The famous San Francisco fog had already begun to roll in. It hovered like a doughnut around the two towers of the Golden Gate Bridge, so that the guys could see the tops of the towers and the traffic underneath, but nothing in between.

San Francisco's seven hills were similarly draped in patches of fog, which left the peaks and valleys clear but clouded up the midsections. Pete thought it was awesome and Jupe tried to analyze the meteorological elements that produced fog every night in the middle of summer.

Then they checked out all of San Francisco's rock radio stations, spinning the dial, listening for a cut by the Stone Bananas, one of Sax's new groups.

When they were only ten or fifteen miles from the airport, however, Pete began to get nervous. He kept glancing in the rear-view mirror and drumming his fingers on the steering wheel.

"Take a look behind us, Jupe," he said. "See a purple Cavalier?"

"I see it," Jupe said. "What about it?"

"I think he's following us," Pete said.

Logic said no. No one knew they had come to San Francisco. It was such a spur of the moment trip. But Pete said yes so strongly. "Okay. Slow down," Jupe said. "We'll take a look."

Pete slowed a little more and the purple car moved up on them, switching to the right lane. Now it was almost even with their back right bumper. Jupe turned to look, but the headlight's bright beam prevented him from seeing the driver's face. Jupe rolled down his window. The driver in the purple car rolled down his window and pulled up a little more. Now he and Jupe were side by side, face to face.

Jupe gasped and jerked back away from the window. It was Mr. Sweetness! He was wearing the army camouflage jacket, his arms bulging in the sleeves. His face was somewhat pockmarked and he held his mouth in a frozen half smile, half sneer. Jupe knew immediately that he was staring into the cold eyes of a killer.

"Let's get out of here!" Jupe shouted.

Pete took his eyes off the road long enough to see exactly what Jupe was shouting about. Mr. Sweetness laughed and suddenly the purple car swerved at them. But Pete stepped on the gas and their rental car jerked ahead.

"He's not just following us. He's trying to smear us across the road," Pete said, taking a quick glance at his mirror.

Mr. Sweetness pulled back into Pete's lane and stayed directly behind him. Every time Pete slowed down for traffic, the purple Cavalier lunged forward and hit them. *Ram!* Hard enough to dent the bumper but not hard enough to mash body metal. *Ram!*

"Take an exit," Jupe said. "We'll lose him!"

Pete pulled off the highway quickly, but so did the Cavalier. No matter how fast Pete drove, the Cavalier was always able to keep up. *Ram!* There didn't seem to be any choice but to keep on driving . . . but for how long? *Ram!*

Both guys realized that being so far away from Rocky

Beach had made them feel safe. The idea that no matter where they went, Mr. Sweetness would be there too, had never occurred to them. Now they were facing that reality . . . alone . . . in the dark . . . *Ram!*

When they reached a remote hillside residential area, Pete turned sharply and aimed the car up a hill. *Ram!* A sign indicated that they were taking a scenic route up to one of San Francisco's most famous tourist attractions—Twin Peaks. From the tops of these two mountains, sightseers had a panoramic view of the water, the city lights, and the entire Bay Area.

But as the road curved upward, Pete found that they were driving right into the doughnut of fog ringing the mountains. *Ram!*

"I've never seen fog like this," Pete said desperately, slowing the car. In fact, it was so thick that they couldn't see more than a foot in front of their headlights. *Ram!* For a moment, Pete thought about turning around and going back down the mountain. But there wasn't room—and they knew Mr. Sweetness wouldn't allow it. *Ram!*

Jupe looked nervously out the back. He couldn't see the Cavalier at all. He couldn't even see another set of headlights. But he *felt* it each time Mr. Sweetness rammed into them.

Then, for what seemed like many minutes, nothing happened.

"Do you think he stopped?" Pete asked Jupe in a tense, thin voice.

"I don't know," Jupe answered. "I can't see a thing. Just keep driving."

Pete gripped the wheel even tighter. They were coming to a curve in the road, and Pete didn't want his concentration to break. It was almost impossible to see the road right in front of the car, let alone the edge where the ground dropped away sharply.

Suddenly, just as Pete was nearing the sharpest part in the curve, the purple Cavalier appeared out of nowhere, driving on the left side of the two-lane road. He was swerving from side to side, trying to push Pete and Jupe over the edge!

"Watch out! We're going over!" Jupe shouted.

Pete pulled the wheel to the left, tires squealed, and they felt the car jerk back onto the pavement from the shoulder. Then Pete held his breath and sped forward blindly. No matter how terrifying it was to drive in this fog, it was better than sticking around for another encounter with Mr. Sweetness.

At the top of the hill the fog disappeared. They had driven high enough to be above it.

With his heart pounding, Pete backed into one of the parking spaces in the curved parking lot overlooking the magnificent vista below. His hands shook as he wiped his forehead.

"Now let's just wait for Mr. Sweetness to show up," Pete said in a furious, let's-get-tough tone of voice.

12

Unwrapping a Clue

PETE AND JUPE SAT SILENTLY ON TOP OF TWIN PEAKS with the motor running. They were waiting for the purple Cavalier with Mr. Sweetness in it to burst through the fog to the top of the hill. Now that they were out of the fog themselves, and surrounded by a few dozen sightseers who could back them up, Pete felt less frightened and a whole lot more angry. In fact, he was burning mad.

"The guy's got a lot of nerve," Pete said, hitting his fist repeatedly on the steering wheel. "I'd like to meet him in a fair fight, I'll tell you that." Pete mentally ran through all the karate moves he knew and would use on Mr. Sweetness if he got the chance. "Why doesn't he show up? What's he doing on that road, anyway?"

"I don't know," Jupe said thoughtfully. "There are a lot of possibilities. . . ."

They waited about thirty minutes and still the Cavalier didn't show up.

Suddenly Jupe slammed his fist into the dashboard. "We've got to get to the airport," he said.

"But what about Mr. Sweetness?" Pete said.

"He's not coming," Jupe said. "He probably turned around and went back down the hill."

Pete slapped the steering wheel with his palms and put the car in gear.

"Look on the bright side," Jupe said. "Now at least we know exactly what he looks like."

Pete drove quickly to the airport and pulled into the Rental Car Returns area. They left the keys in the car, as instructed, and then rushed into the rental office to pay. But just before they got to the office, Pete spun Jupe around by the arm.

"Look!" he said, pointing to a returned car parked near the front.

"A purple Cavalier!" Jupe exclaimed. "But is it the one we're looking for?"

They walked over and circled the empty car.

"It's the right license plate," said Jupe. "Quick! Go into the office and see if he's still in there, and stall him. If he's not there, try to find out from the clerks what Mr. Sweetness's real name is. I'll be there to help you in a minute."

As Pete left, Jupe opened the purple car's passenger door and leaned inside. Was there something in the car that might be a clue? Jupe started searching, meticulously checking the carpeting behind, under, and in front of the seats. He checked the ashtrays and the glove compartment, and even squeezed his hand into the narrow space between the pedals to check under the floor mats. Then he stood up, puffing a little from being bent over for so long.

But it had been worth it. He had found something, something crucial. It didn't tell him who Mr. Sweetness was. But it told him the next best thing—where he might go to find out. Jupe rushed to the rental office and met Pete coming out.

"What did the clerk say?" asked Jupe.

"Have a nice day," Pete said.

"About the purple car," Jupe said impatiently.

"Have a nice day," Pete repeated. "That's all it says. It's a computer."

"Look what I found," Jupe said, pulling out a small crumpled piece of paper, shiny foil on one side and plain white on the other.

"A candy wrapper," Pete said, smoothing it until he could read the name written in silver ink. "Miracle Tastes! It's like the candy Don Dellasandro handed out at Big Barney's party!"

"Yes, exactly," Jupe said. "Free samples of a product *not* on the market yet. This creates two possibilities. Mr. Sweetness could have been at the party and gotten candy samples as we all did. Or—and this would be considerably more interesting—perhaps Don Dellasandro and Mr. Sweetness are in league together."

"We're just a plane ride from finding out," Pete said. "Let's go home!"

It was midnight when Jupe returned to the junkyard and too late to do anything except work on his latest electronic project—the lock combination decoder. When he got too tired to tinker with it anymore, he turned off the workshop light and started to lock up.

Just then the phone rang.

"Hello?" Jupe said in the darkness.

"Hello, Jupe, it's Pete. Kelly wants to talk to you. Tell him, babe."

Jupe flipped the lights back on.

"Hi, Jupe!" Kelly said with an awful lot of energy. "Well . . . like . . . you know, Juliet Coop took me out to lunch today . . ." she began.

Jupe could picture Kelly twisting one long brown piece of hair, and he knew this was going to be a long story. He put the call on the speaker phone so he could walk around while he listened.

". . . but she doesn't remember where she was or where her briefcase might be," Kelly was saying. "But she remembers something about a car behind her that night . . . but it's still fuzzy. Anyway, after lunch she gave me a ride home, and it was great. Big Barney just gave her a new Mustang convertible."

"You know the one," Pete interrupted in the background. "The baby with the five-liter V-8 engine and the—"

"Pete, please," Kelly said. "Jupe wants to hear this story. So anyway, where was I? Oh, yeah. So before she got in the car, she opened the trunk and threw in her purse. Hey, I said to myself, that was weird. So I asked her, 'What'd you do that for?' 'Habit,' she said. She was riding with the top down once in her old Mustang and someone reached in and grabbed her purse. So do you get the picture, Jupe?"

Jupe's eyes lit up. The trunk! Juliet's briefcase might be in her trunk!

"Yes! A brilliant observation, Kelly. You're learning a lot from me," Jupe said.

Kelly sort of snorted a laugh.

"Let me talk to Pete," Jupe said. "Pete, first thing Monday morning, we're going to the auto salvage yard to check out the trunk of Juliet's car."

"Knew you'd say that," said Pete. "Okay, see ya."

At 9:00 Monday morning, Pete and Bob showed up in the VW. But Jupe wasn't quite ready. He picked up the phone and dialed the number of police headquarters. When Chief Reynolds got on the line, Jupe announced he was calling about Juliet Coop's briefcase.

"A briefcase is news to me," said the chief.

"Of course, you searched the scene of the accident thoroughly for all personal property," Jupe said.

"Of course," the chief answered patiently.

"And the car?" asked Jupe.

"Jupiter, I have uniforms that are older than you are," said Chief Reynolds. "I know how to do my job. My guys said the car was empty."

"I was just checking loose ends," Jupe said.

"Grasping at straws, you mean. You wouldn't want to put a little wager on this case, would you, Jupiter?"

asked Chief Reynolds with a laugh. "Loser buys the winner a Big Barney dinner?"

"Chief, if I lose this one, Big Barney's chicken may be the last thing you'd want to eat," Jupe said. "Talk to you later."

Then Jupe joined his friends and the Three Investigators drove over to the Miller Auto Wreckage Yard. It was the size of two city blocks and surrounded by a tall wooden fence. The far side of the yard was piled high with newly wrecked cars just waiting to be stripped. Scattered elsewhere throughout the lot were piles of various sorts: tires, fenders, cars that were too damaged to be used for parts, and so on. In the left rear corner of the lot there was a huge compactor machine and a 200-foot crane.

Almost as if it had been planned by a television action-adventure show writer, they arrived at the exact moment when Juliet's little blue Mustang was being lifted into the air by the enormous electromagnet on the end of the crane.

"He's going to drop it in the masher!" Pete shouted. "It'll squeeze the metal into a solid block!"

"We'll never get anything out of the trunk then," Bob said, breaking into a run.

They ran as fast as they could to the crane, shouting and waving at the crane operator. When they got there, they saw it was Dick Miller, the owner's son, who had just graduated from Rocky Beach High School a year ago.

He shut down the motor and stepped out on the big yellow painted platform around the operator's cage. "What's your problem?" he shouted down to them.

"If that's Juliet Coop's car, we've got to see it," Jupe shouted back.

"That's it, all right," Dick Miller said. "But it's past it for spare parts, guys."

"We only need to inspect it for a minute," Jupe said.

"Okay, I'll set it down over there," Dick Miller said, pointing to a space in the middle of the yard beside a huge pile of trucks.

The Three Investigators nodded and headed for the area where Dick Miller had pointed. As they walked the crane's engine started up again and the wrecked car, dangling at the end of the flat, round magnet, started moving after them. Jupe looked over his shoulder and saw the car swinging gently back and forth. But then it began to pick up speed, swinging in wider arcs.

"That thing's gonna really hit hard when it hits the ground," Pete said. "He's crazy."

They moved back out of the way but the car above them followed, swinging dangerously near.

"What's the joke?" Pete shouted above the roar of the crane's engine.

"It's no joke! Look!" Bob shouted.

On the ground at the foot of the crane lay Dick Miller. He was holding his stomach, doubled over in pain. Someone else had climbed up into the crane operator's booth and was now working the controls. The crane swung the car ten feet above their heads.

"Who's operating the crane?" Jupe asked.

But there wasn't time for an answer. Suddenly the crane swung the car toward them, and then the electromagnet let go of Juliet's car. All 3,000 pounds of mangled metal came falling to the ground.

13

A (Brief) Case for Murder

THE CAR HIT THE GROUND WITH A SHATTERING crash. Fortunately the Three Investigators had dodged just in time. They crouched behind a stack of wrecked cars, watching the empty electromagnet swing freely in space. All by itself, the magnet was big enough and heavy enough to knock a person dead. And it was obvious that whoever was in the operator's booth wouldn't mind that kind of "accident" one bit.

When the giant magnet stopped swinging, Pete peeked out from his hiding place to see who was in the crane's cab.

"I should have known," he whispered to his buddies. "It's Mr. Sweetness."

All three Investigators came out from behind the stack of cars. They saw a tall man in army camouflage fatigues climbing out of the cab of the crane. He jumped down and gave Dick Miller a chop to the back of the neck to keep him from getting up.

"He's coming this way," Pete said, motioning to his friends to back away. The three of them ducked around to the other side of the car pile, trying to stay out of sight.

"He probably wants to get into Juliet's car—just like we do," Jupe said.

Suddenly they heard a bottle break followed by a sharp crackling sound. Pete didn't look out again until he smelled the smoke. When he looked, he saw Mr. Sweetness tossing a second Molotov cocktail into Juliet's car.

"He's destroying the evidence!" Pete said frantically.

"So that's it," Jupe said. "He doesn't want what's in the car. He just wants to make sure *we* don't get it!"

"If there's still gas in the tank, that car will go off like a skyrocket!" Pete said.

As soon as the flames took hold, Mr. Sweetness ran for his Porsche at the entrace of the junkyard. Pete started to follow, but Bob and Jupe held him back.

"Never mind him," Bob said, grabbing Pete's arm forcefully. "We've got to get into that trunk!"

"Quick, before Juliet's car burns up!" Jupe added.

"*Explodes*, you mean!" Bob said.

Pete took one look at Juliet's flaming car and flew into action. He raced around the junkyard, looking in open car trunks and digging through piles. Finally he found what he needed—an old crowbar. Then he rushed to Juliet's bombed-out Mustang. The flames had already eaten away most of the interior and were working their way toward the back—where the gas tank was.

Sweat flew off Pete's forehead as he applied the crowbar to the trunk, all the while keeping an eye on the flames. Finally the trunk lid gave up and sprang open.

"Got it!" Pete called triumphantly as he reached inside and pulled out a soft brown leather briefcase. He waved it in the air for Jupe and Bob to see. "Let's get out of here before this thing blows!" he cried.

Jupe smiled. "Being very familiar with the rules and regulations of junkyards, I know for a fact that gas tanks of wrecked cars are drained," he said to Bob. "The car's not going to blow up."

"Why didn't you tell me that before?" Pete asked, giving Jupe an exasperated glare.

"I knew by the time I'd convinced you it was really safe, the car would have burned up," Jupe said. "You work better when your raw instincts take over."

"Thanks a lot." Pete groaned.

After calling an ambulance, Jupe, Bob, and Pete hung around to make certain that Dick Miller was going to be all right.

"I always heard you guys were detectives," Dick Miller said. "But I didn't know you investigated bombers and stuff like that."

"It's not always this rough," Jupe said with an apologetic smile.

Then they hurried to Big Barney's mansion, where Juliet and Kelly were waiting for them. Big Barney himself was out and not expected home until late.

"Did you find anything?" the two anxious girls said at once as they opened the front door.

Jupe merely held up the briefcase as evidence of the morning's adventure.

Juliet smiled and led the way into the living room, where Jupe laid the briefcase down on the glass coffee table. Eagerly she unzipped the front compartment and pulled out her blue morocco-leather appointment book. She turned to the page that listed her plans for that fateful Friday—the day of her accident, the day that was so blank in her memory.

"Here it is," she said, breathing quickly.

She stared at the page for a minute and then shook her head. "All it says for the whole day is R&D."

"That's Research and Development, Pandro Mishkin's department, isn't it?" Jupe said. "Why would you have been meeting with him?"

"I was spending a whole day in each department, to learn the business," Juliet said. "But I don't remember anything more."

"Maybe you will when you see what else is inside the briefcase," Jupe urged.

Juliet opened the back leather flap and found a three-ring binder with about two hundred xeroxed pages in it. She took it out and flipped through the pages for a few minutes, then dropped it and shrugged. "I don't recognize this material," she said. It was clear that she had been counting on getting her memory of the accident back when the briefcase was found. She was terribly disappointed.

"Do you mind if I have a look?" Jupe said. He picked up the notebook. Pandro Mishkin's name was stamped on the first page. Quickly Jupe scanned the report.

After reading silently for a few minutes, Jupe looked up and addressed the room.

"I believe I can now reconstruct much of what must have happened two Fridays ago, the night of Juliet's accident," he began. "This is Pandro Mishkin's copy of a report about a food additive called Multisorbitane. It was invented by Don Dellasandro several years ago. In the summary it says that Multisorbitane, as a food enhancer, makes foods taste remarkably better and more intense—but there's a catch. It makes food so good, in fact, it's nearly addicting."

"Is that the catch?" Bob asked.

"Surprisingly, it isn't," Jupe said. "The FDA—the Federal Food and Drug Administation—tested Multisorbitane, as it must test all new drugs and products of this nature. But it denied Don Dellasandro permission to market Multisorbitane because it found strong evidence that it might be a carcinogen."

"A what?" asked Pete.

"It could cause cancer," Bob explained.

Jupe cleared his throat and continued. "We know that you met with Pandro Mishkin on the Friday of your accident. And we know that you have his copy of this incriminating report in your possession. Now we move from what we know," he said, tapping the report, "to what we *think* we know. I suspect that you discovered this report, perhaps by accident, sometime during your visit to Mishkin's office. Considering the time of your accident, I'd say it was late in the day when you found it. And when you did, I think it upset you quite a bit," Jupe said.

Jupe was pacing now, going into high gear. "I think it upset you so much that you took it from Pandro Mishkin's office and fled. He probably chased you to get it back. And when you left the Chicken Coop Corp. building in your car, I think that Pandro Mishkin followed you. In short, I believe it was he who was driving the car that left the second set of tracks at the scene of your accident."

"Time out," Pete said. "Why did this report upset Juliet so much?"

"Yes, that is the key question, isn't it?" Jupe said, smiling knowingly. "It upset her because she knew, or suspected, as I do, that Multisorbitane is a key ingredient in a delicious new product called Drippin' Chicken!"

Jupe let them all digest that idea for a moment and then he began again. "You discovered the horrible fact that someone—maybe Pandro, maybe Dellasandro, maybe even your father—was knowingly and quite cold-bloodedly putting this poison into Drippin' Chicken. Of course the effects of the Multisorbitane wouldn't show up for years. But slowly, over a period of time, millions of people who had regularly eaten this carcinogen would begin to get cancer. No one would realize the danger until it was too late."

Juliet's mouth was trembling. "My father wouldn't do something like that!" she cried out.

"We can't really know that—unless you can help us prove it," Jupe said without missing a beat.

It was clear to everyone that his mind, as usual, was working well ahead of the conversation.

"What kind of scheme do you have in mind, Jupe?" Bob asked.

"It's simple," Jupe said. "We've got to find out if Big Barney knows about the Multisorbitane in the Drippin' Chicken recipe. Any idea how we can do that?"

"I know how," said Juliet. "My father keeps the recipes for his products in a safe in his office."

Jupe snapped his fingers. "I was hoping he did. Can you get it for us?"

"I don't know the combination of the safe," she replied. "Only Big Barney knows it."

"Well, that's no good," Jupe said. "We have to get the recipe without Big Barney knowing it. He can't suspect what we're doing."

Juliet suddenly smiled. "How about Dad's secretary?" Juliet asked. "She probably knows more about him than he does. She might know the combination."

"Let's go," Pete said.

"No. I want to go by myself," said Juliet. "I'm not even sure I should be doing this. Dad's recipes are top secret—you'll have to promise . . ."

"Of course, of course," Jupe said. "Now, when do you think we can expect you?"

"A couple of hours," said Juliet.

Two hours came and went. The Three Investigators and Kelly spent the time doing what Juliet had suggested. Eat her food, watch her TV, relax. The third one was too difficult for Jupiter.

Another hour passed.

Finally the door opened and Juliet came in, carrying a piece of paper and giving everyone a large smile.

"I've got the recipe," she whispered, looking around to be sure her father wasn't home. "There's no mention of Multisorbitane in Drippin' Chicken's ingredients. See? My dad isn't some kind of crazed killer."

Jupe grabbed the paper quickly and started reading it.

"Looks like our case is going down the tubes," Pete said.

Jupe folded the paper and put it in his pocket. Then he looked at Juliet. "If no one is poisoning the chicken, then why did you say so in your sleep? And why was it so important to you to find your briefcase? And why was this report about Multisorbitane, with Pandro Mishkin's stamp, in your possession?"

"I don't know," said Juliet.

"We don't know either," Jupe said solemnly. "But there are a few things we do know. For one, our list of suspects is shrinking rapidly. Your father seems to be out. Michael Argenti is out, because we have nothing to connect him with Multisorbitane or with this report from Pandro Mishkin. Pandro himself is a question mark. He could be innocent, he could be involved. But the suspect I'm most interested in is the person who didn't want us to find this report . . . the person who sent Mr. Sweetness to scare us off . . . the person who invented Drippin' Chicken in the first place. Don Dellasandro!"

"What now?" Kelly asked. "Call the police?"

"No. We need proof," Jupe said. "We've got to get into Miracle Tastes and find out exactly what Don Dellasandro is hiding."

"Jupe, the place is a Class A security nightmare," Pete warned.

"Okay, then we'll have to go in there late tonight," said Jupe, "when the guards are half asleep."

"You'd better make that early tonight," Juliet said. "My dad's secretary reminded me of something else I forgot. There's a big press party planned for this evening. Big Barney is going to introduce Drippin' Chicken to the world! Everyone will be eating the stuff."

"Oh, no!" Kelly exclaimed.

Remembering Big Barney's own words, Jupe said, "The American people won't know what hit them!"

14

The Secret Ingredient

AT 5:00 P.M. THE INVESTIGATORS WERE SITTING IN Bob's car, parked inconspicuously across the road from the Miracle Tastes office and warehouse building in Long Beach. They had stopped first at home to change into black jeans and black T-shirts. Jupe also brought with him a small, mysterious black leather case, which he held carefully on his lap. It was something Pete and Bob had never seen before.

"As soon as Dellasandro leaves, we make our move," Jupe said, cradling the black box.

"How do we know he's in there?" Bob asked.

"His car is there," Pete said. "I recognize it."

"When did you see it?" Bob asked, surprised.

"After the taping of Big Barney's new commercial. I followed Big Barney, remember?" Pete said. "And he came here, to Miracle Tastes."

Little by little, the parking lot at Miracle Tastes emptied out. But it wasn't until 6:00 P.M. that Don Dellasandro's gray Cadillac Allanté rolled out and headed up the road toward L.A.

"He's probably going to Big Barney's press party," Pete said.

They got out of the car and ran across the nearly empty Miracle Tastes parking lot. When they reached the entrance, Bob kept watch as Pete and Jupe examined the door.

"Will you look at that security system?" Pete moaned.

All six of their eyes focused on a small electronic panel with a lighted keypad. It was located on the chrome wall beside the glass doorway. Just inside the door was a security guard's station, but no one was there.

"He's probably still making rounds," Bob concluded. "Let's make this snappy."

From the look of the keypad, the Three Investigators decided that it worked something like their own security system at Headquarters. A special combination had to be entered on the keypad before the door would open. But who knew what would happen if the wrong codes were entered?

Jupe unzipped his small black leather case. "Luckily for us, I've been constructing an electronic lock combination decoder for weeks," Jupe said. "Once I connect the decoder to the keypad, my device will read the combination. I've tried it at Headquarters and it works."

Jupe quickly unscrewed the cover plate to the keypad and attached the decoder's two alligator clips to two special wires in the security system. His heart was pounding. He flipped a switch, and after some beeps and flashes the decoder gave Jupe a combination of numbers.

"Okay, let's try it," Pete said, moving toward the door.

But Jupe grabbed Pete's shoulder. "Wait! Something's wrong." Jupe nervously fiddled with the black decoder.

"I'll say it is," Bob agreed when he looked at Jupe's device. "It's giving you the wrong combination. That's the combination of *our* security system at Headquarters!"

Jupe flushed red with embarrassment. "There must be a flaw in the capacitor . . . or the impedence could be incorrectly calculated . . . ahh, I'm sorry, guys."

"Don't worry about it," Bob said. "Just put that thing away—quick! Here comes the guard."

Jupe stuffed the decoder in his shirt and the three of them tried to look casual as the security guard approached the front desk. Before he got there, Bob reached up and rang the night bell.

The guard opened the door only a crack, eyeing them up and down. "What can I do for you?" he asked cautiously.

Jupe was determined to make up for his failure with the lock decoder.

"Three Guys in Black T-Shirts Messenger Service," Jupe said. "We're supposed to pick up something in

Mr. Dellasandro's office. He said it was a matter of life and death."

"It takes three guys to pick up a package?" asked the guard suspiciously.

"Well, I've got the job," Jupe said.

"But I own the car," added Bob.

"And I have a road map," said Pete.

"I thought the Three Stooges were dead," muttered the guard. He opened the door and let them in. "Get your package and get out of here." He motioned impatiently toward a hall.

The Three Investigators followed the guard's directions, taking the carpeted hallway to the left, which led to offices, rather than the concrete hallway to the right.

At the end of the hallway they came to a large walnut door marked EXECUTIVE SUITE.

Don Dellasandro's office was spacious, with ceiling-to-floor windows on two sides. It smelled of fresh-cut flowers, even though there wasn't a single bloom in the room. The central feature of the room was a large rosewood desk with a built-in telephone and computer. There was also Nautilus exercise equipment in one corner. All over the walls were mementos and awards from Dellasandro's past flavoring achievements. Labels from candy bars, salad dressings, babies' rubber pacifiers, frozen mixed eggplant and zucchini, and more were framed and displayed.

The awards didn't impress Jupiter, but the thoroughness of Don Dellasandro's filing system did.

"What are we looking for?" Pete asked, going through Dellasandro's king-size executive desk.

"A jar of Multisorbitane would be helpful," Jupe said, opening another file cabinet. "But I'll settle for any evidence that Don Dellasandro has tampered with the ingredients of Drippin' Chicken." Jupe's fingers flipped through one file folder after another.

"He has a computer terminal in his executive washroom," Bob said from the bathroom, trying a splash of one of Dellasandro's expensive men's colognes. He reappeared in the room. "Does it make me smell like a million?"

"A million what?" Pete asked.

"Brominated pseudophosphates!" Jupe exclaimed.

"Watch your language, Jupe," Bob said. "Pete's at an impressionable age."

"Brominated pseudophosphates is one of the ingredients in Drippin' Chicken," Jupe said. "At least, according to the recipe Juliet got for us."

"It sounds more like something Pete put in my car engine last week," Bob said.

Jupe slammed the file cabinet closed. "But I have just gone through two years' worth of purchase orders, invoices, and inventory lists. There's no evidence that Miracle Tastes has purchased or manufactured any of that ingredient! We've got to get into the warehouse immediately."

They ran back down the carpeted hall and found the same security guard, dozing at the front desk. He woke up with a start. "Get your package?" he asked.

Pete and Bob looked to Jupe to supply an answer.

"No," Jupe said. "He said it would be right here in the warehouse office, but it wasn't."

"Warehouse office?" sputtered the guard. "That isn't the warehouse! Does this look like a warehouse? Don't any of you boys have any common sense?"

"The fourth guy has common sense," Bob said. "But he didn't want to come tonight."

"Go down that concrete hallway. Walk through three red doors. *That's* the warehouse," said the guard. "Do you know what a door looks like?"

"He does," Pete said, pointing to Jupe.

Down the hall, through three red doors, the Investigators found themselves catching their breath in a cavernous room filled with pyramids of sealed drums full of chemicals.

"Spread out and check every label," Jupe said.

"What time is it?" Bob called.

"Almost seven."

"Don't forget the press party starts at nine," Bob reminded them. "We've got to hurry."

Pete and Bob wandered separately up and down the aisles, surrounded by drums of powdered acids.

"Hey, guys, over here!" Bob suddenly called.

Pete and Jupe worked their way through the maze of barrels to reach Bob. Their shoes squeaked on the clean, painted concrete floor. They found Bob standing in front of a stack of barrels. Each one was marked in big letters BROMINATED PSEUDOPHOSPHATES.

"Here's what you're looking for, Jupe," Bob said. "But what does it prove?"

Jupiter examined the barrels carefully. "Look at the received dates on the barrels," Jupe said.

"They came in a couple of months ago," Pete said.

"How could they?" asked Jupe. "I just went through his invoices. They clearly indicate that in the last two years he hasn't ordered or stocked a single pound, a single ounce of brominated pseudophosphates. Let's get a sample out of these drums. I'd like to know what's *really* in them."

"Bottom line? I think you can guess the answer to that question," said a voice behind them.

The Investigators whirled around. Don Dellasandro stood behind them.

"I was hoping we wouldn't have to interface like this," he said. "I was hoping that you'd drop the ball on this investigation, but instead you're impacting on me—negatively."

The guys froze in fear.

"I'm sorry," Don Dellasandro said, drawing a gun from his pocket. He aimed the gun at the Investigators, at about heart level. "You guys are expendable. I've got to waste you."

15

A Taste of Fear

HOLDING HIS GUN ON THE DETECTIVES, DON Dellasandro quickly looked at his watch. "Okay, there's a little time before Big Barney's party at the Beverly Hilton." He reached into his other jacket pocket.

What now? thought Jupe.

Slowly Dellasandro pulled his hand out of his jacket, but he kept the hand closed. "We can network for a few minutes," he said. "Want to do some market research before you go belly up?"

"What do you mean?" asked Jupe, staring hard at Dellasandro's fist.

He opened his hand. He had more wrapped candies. "Try one," he said.

"It's poison, Jupe," Pete warned.

"Would I poison someone with taste buds like his? It's a shame I have to kill you, pal."

Jupe looked at Dellasandro, then at the gun, then at the candy, then at the clock on the wall. What good would it do to stall? The police weren't on their way. No one was coming to rescue them.

"I'd really value your input," Dellasandro said. "Unless you're in a big hurry to die. Tell me what you taste. Are my flavors on target?"

"Okay," Jupe said reluctantly. "I'll try it. But it's going to cost you."

"Everything has a price," Dellasandro said. "I used to think being a scientist was a noble profession. But without marketing skills it's just bottle pouring or germ breeding. Today if you can't tune into your channels, what good are you?"

"You can always get hooked up to cable," Bob said.

"Watch it!" Dellasandro said, suddenly wheeling toward Bob in anger. "I *hate* people who treat business like a joke! You're lucky your friend here is such a genius in the taste bud department, or you'd already be dead meat." He took two deep breaths to calm himself down and then added, "Dead meat is one of my best flavors, by the way."

Jupe held very still, as it dawned on him that Dellasandro was more than a little unhinged. Maybe he'd ingested too much Multisorbitane over the years.

"I'll try a piece of candy," Jupe said calmly. "But only on one condition. You've got to answer a question."

Dellasandro nodded and handed Jupe the candy. Jupe popped it into his mouth.

"Three tastes," Jupe said. "Lemon—real lemon essence, not imitation—meringue, and graham cracker crust. It's lemon meringue pie."

"Phenomenal," Dellasandro said.

"Now my turn," Jupe said. "This is Multisorbitane in these drums, the ones marked 'brominated pseudophosphates,' isn't it?"

"It is," Dellasandro said. "So what?"

"So what are you planning to use it for? I'm quite sure you know that it's an unacceptable food additive as far as the FDA is concerned."

"You want to ask another question? First you eat another candy. Pick one," Dellasandro said with a devilish grin. He held out his hand for Jupe to choose.

"Don't do it, Jupe. It's a trick," Pete said.

Jupe didn't really think the candy was poison, but he *did* think it might have Multisorbitane in it. Nonetheless, he had no choice. He wanted a confession from Dellasandro, and he wanted more time. He took a foil-wrapped candy from Dellasandro and tasted it.

"Cherry Jell-O with banana floaters and whipped cream," Jupe said, chomping down on the sample bonbon. "I've answered your question. Now answer mine. What are you going to do with these drums of Multisorbitane?"

Dellasandro took his time about answering. Finally he said, "Okay. I'll tell you—since we all know you won't be alive long enough to repeat it. Let me background a little. About a year ago, Big Barney Coop came to me. He wanted to collaborate on a new product, something no one had seen, tasted, or dreamed before—especially not Michael Argenti. He said he'd divide the profits with me and we were talking a dollar sign and then zeros off the page. But there were two conditions. One: the gravy had to be *in* the chicken. Two: it had to be sensationally delicious."

"Did Big Barney say to make it deadly?" Bob asked.

"*You* shut up!" Dellasandro shouted at Bob. More deep-breathing exercises. Then he was calm again. "Getting the gravy into the chicken turned out to be easy," Dellasandro continued. "Freeze-dried gravy injected as powder into the chicken fillets. When the chicken is fried at the restaurant, the gravy reconstitutes itself. The second puzzle was harder. How to irresistibilize the product. I tried every flavor, flavor savor, flavor enhancer, flavor duplicator I could think of for the gravy. They were good, but they weren't perfect."

"So you used Multisorbitane?" Jupe asked.

Dellasandro handed Jupe a third piece of candy. "Time was running out," he said, checking his watch. "I couldn't think of anything else to put in the gravy. My reputation and all those zeros after the dollar sign were at risk." Then Dellasandro noticed that Jupe wasn't eating the third candy. "What's the matter— are you *full*?"

"I'm saving it for dessert," Jupe said.

"Jupe, just remember he put a carcinogen into Drippin' Chicken," Bob warned.

"The cancer won't impact on people for ten or

twenty years," Dellasandro said. "That's a long time. No one will know. Big Barney won't know because I'm on the supply side of the gravy powder for his food processors. They'll send the prepared chicken to the restaurants, who interface with the customers directly. Everybody's happy, which is, after all, the highest goal of our civilization today."

Jupe looked at the clock on the wall again. It was almost eight, and he was almost out of ideas. His first analysis had been right: there was no point in stalling. Still, the impulse to buy more time was a hard one to ignore.

"I have one more question, if you'll allow me," Jupe said. "What made you come back here tonight?"

"I pay my security team well," Dellasandro replied. "The guard networked with me on my car phone as soon as you guys showed up." He looked at the last candy, which was still in Jupe's hand. "Eat your dessert, pal, because the bottom line is, your quality time is up."

Jupe unwrapped the candy. This one was different. It was hard and heavy in his hand. "Mr. Sweetness works for you, doesn't he?" said Jupe. "The guy in the army jacket."

"Mr. Sweetness?" Dellasandro laughed. "Highly original. Yeah, Vinnie's my next-door neighbor. Got a pink slip from the marines, I understand. They seemed to think he was too vicious to be a real team player. The moment Juliet mentioned at Big Barney's party that you were detectives, I strategized that Vin-

nie could help me scare you guys off. I told him to do
whatever he had to do. First he tapped your phone."

"So that's how he knew we ordered Chinese food,"
Jupe realized.

"Yeah, he took the ball and ran with it. I was very
impressed with his creativity. But somehow you kept
getting away from him." Dellasandro waved his gun
toward Jupe's mouth. "Eat the candy," he said.

"Don't do it, Jupe," Pete warned.

Jupe slowly put the candy into his mouth. After a
moment, he said, "Caramel."

"Just wait," said Don Dellasandro, smiling.

Jupe chewed some more and then said, "Oh, very
clever. It's caramel apple. Now I can taste the apple."

"Mr. Sweetness—that's what I'll call that flavor,"
Dellasandro said. "I'll flash on you every time someone says it."

"You're a brilliant scientist, a clever marketing
man, but a terrible killer," said Jupe.

"In this new age we can't always do what we like,
but we have to do what's important," Dellasandro
replied. "In my mind I can image myself wasting you
three."

"Not with the safety catch locked on your gun," said
Jupe.

"It is?" Dellasandro said, looking down.

Pete didn't wait. He moved instinctively into a flying
yoko-tobi-geri side kick, connecting with Dellasandro's
hand. The gun flew into the air and clattered on the
ground.

Then Pete and Bob both charged Dellasandro, but the older man was strong and quick. He seemed to know some karate moves too. He gave Bob a quick kick in the knee, which sent Bob down. Then Dellasandro spun and arced a ridge hand at Pete. Pete blocked the blow and gave Dellasandro a *gyaku-tsuki* reverse punch to the ribs. The scientist winced and staggered backward. Pete leaped into the air, twisting and lifting his feet high.

"*Aiiiya,*" Pete screamed, knocking Dellasandro down.

But Dellasandro rolled and stood up. He looked around. Then he saw the gun on the floor a second before Jupe did. He rushed to grab it. "I'm terminating this meeting!" he shouted.

16

Big Barney Wings It

DELLASANDRO DOVE FOR THE REVOLVER. JUPE grabbed frantically for it at the same time, but he was just a moment too late. Dellasandro actually laughed when he picked up the gun. Then he stood up to face the Three Investigators.

It wasn't until then that Dellasandro realized he had paid too much attention to the gun—and too little attention to the three guys he was fighting. Because just then a heavy drum marked BROMINATED PSEUDO-PHOSPHATES, but actually filled with Multisorbitane, came flying through the air.

Pete and Bob had lifted it together and heaved it at Dellasandro. The drum hit him like a wrecking ball, knocking him down and out. It burst open when it struck the floor, dumping hundreds of pounds of Multisorbitane over everything, even on the chemist who had invented it.

"Talk about getting a taste of your own medicine," Bob said with a whistle.

Pete and Jupe quickly tied up Dellasandro with extension cords. Shortly Dellasandro began to regain consciousness.

"What happened?" Dellasandro asked groggily.

"You didn't miss much," Jupe replied. "You gave us a full confession and then there was a fight and you lost. Now you're tied up."

"There's no time to call the police," Bob said. "We'll have to catch them later tonight."

"Police?" Dellasandro echoed.

"Yes," Jupe said. "We're pressing charges for your small indiscretion in hiring someone to follow us, trying to market an illegal food additive, and threatening to kill us. I think at least one of those charges will stick. But first we've got to get to the Beverly Hilton Hotel. Come on, you guys."

It was a half-hour drive, cut shorter by the fact that Pete drove. They pulled up in front of the hotel and ran through the lobby. The press party, a sign said, was about to begin in the Empire Ballroom.

The Investigators ran past the ballroom entrances and headed right for the kitchen. There they found Big Barney in a yellow jogging suit covered with orange and red feathers. Juliet and Pandro Mishkin were standing by him. And almost every inch of kitchen counter space was covered with steaming trays of Drippin' Chicken.

"Hey, guy," Big Barney said as soon as he saw Jupe. He wrapped his arm around Jupe's shoulder. "Tell me the truth, even though I may never speak to you again and will probably try to ruin your life if I don't like the answer—is this outfit too conservative?"

"Big Barney, forget about your outfit. You can't go out there," Jupe said. "Drippin' Chicken is deadly. It's filled with a dangerous carcinogen. You've got to cancel this party and withdraw the product—or millions of people will die."

Big Barney stared at Jupe and the noisy, clattering kitchen fell silent. Then suddenly Big Barney burst into laughter. "Hahahaha! You almost had me. I'm telling you I've got to have this guy for my son."

"Look! Mishkin's getting away!" Bob shouted.

Everyone did look. And what they saw was Pandro Mishkin trying to sprint out of the kitchen.

Pete and Bob and Jupe immediately grabbed the first thing they could get their hands on. It was a long baker's tray piled high with Drippin' Chicken. They heaved it at the fleeing man, hitting him in the back. Drippin' Chicken splattered everywhere. Then Pete made a diving leap, grabbed Pandro Mishkin at the shoulders, and brought him down in a smear of gravy, like a wide receiver in the mud.

"Complete and utter insubordination!" Mishkin yelled, struggling with Pete. "You could be court-martialed for this."

"It's you who will be going to court, Mr. Mishkin," Jupe said, "for poisoning the Drippin' Chicken."

"Torture me if you want but all you'll get is my name, rank, and serial number. I won't talk," Mishkin said proudly.

"You don't really have to," Jupe said. "Don Della-sandro told us just about everything we need to know—including how you paid him to poison Big Barney's chicken."

"The lying traitor!" cried Mishkin. "*He* paid *me!*"

Jupe couldn't help smiling. "You're right," he said. "My mistake."

"What are you talking about, Mishkin?" Big Barney asked, his eyes wide with disbelief. "Give me your report!"

"General," Pandro answered, "your Drippin' Chicken is filled with an additive the FDA outlawed a few years ago. How do you like them apples?"

"You betrayed me?" Big Barney boomed.

"You didn't pay me a million dollars. And Don Dellasandro did," Mishkin replied.

"And all you had to do was falsify the ingredients of Drippin' Chicken," said Jupe.

"A million bucks buys a lot of loyalty from this soldier," Mishkin said. "I should have gone mercenary a long time ago."

Big Barney rushed over to Mishkin and tore the chicken medals off his jacket. "I'd like to wring your neck!" Big Barney shouted.

Jupe stepped between them and asked one more question. "*You* were the one chasing Juliet Coop the night of her accident, weren't you?"

"Correct," Mishkin said.

"Why, Mr. Mishkin?" asked Juliet. She held her father's arm tightly, as if needing the support.